Lincoln's Doctor's Dog

& other stories
by Richard Grayson

WHITE EWE PRESS

Acknowledgments:
The stories in this collection have appeared in the following
magazines: *American Man, Apalachee Quarterly, Aspect,
Canadian Jewish Dialog, Coffee Break, First Person Intense,
Foothill Quarterly, Gargoyle, Interstate, Iron, Junction,
Mississippi Mud, Nantucket Review, Panache, Penny Dreadful, RiverSedge, Scholia Satyrica, Snakeroots, Sou'wester,
Syzygy, Texas Quarterly, Transatlantic Review.*

Artwork by Boris Milutinovich.

For Lola Szladits and Liz Smith.

ISBN: 0-917976-13-4
Library of Congress
Cataloging in Publication No.: 81-69117

Published by:
The White Ewe Press
P.O. Box 996
Adelphi, Md. 20783

CONTENTS

APPEARANCE HOUSE

There
   is a photograph of me taken on my sixteenth birthday.
Sivia took it at the park. I am crouching by a London plane
tree. I am smiling. There is a sprinkling of acne at one corner
of my mouth but I am freshly sunburned. My eyes are blue.
My hair is blonder than it has ever been since. The shirt I am
wearing is robin's egg blue. It has two buttons which are un-
buttoned. There is a round St. Christopher's medal on my
chest. I look like I have just eaten a Hershey's chocolate bar.
I am smiling. My mind is thinking about a performance of
"A Midsummer's Night Dream" which I have just seen, a performance Sivia has taken me to see. The play was performed
by teenagers and of course I had fallen in love with the boy
playing Lysander. Or with the girl playing Hermia. It had to
be one of those two. I am smiling. There is a red sun in front
of my eyes so perhaps I am squinting, but in any case I am
smiling as well. Sivia is watching me so of course I am smiling. That is my sixteenth-birthday photograph.

There was
   a time when I was a foolish enough child to believe
that where I lived was A Parent's House. Once I wrote it
down like that on the return address of an envelope contain-

ing a letter to my pen-pal Mansarde Garrett, a pen-pal a computer picked out for me at the World's Fair. Sivia noticed the spelling of A Parent's House and would have laughed herself silly had not silliness been a feeling that Sivia could never have.

"It's not A Parent's House," Sivia told me. Then she wrote it down for me on the back of a prescription for laetrile. "Appearance House. This is where you live, boy. Appearance House. You must remember that and be proud of it."

So I rewrote the letter to my pen-pal and stuck it into a new envelope that Sivia gave me, some of her own robin's egg blue stationery.

Through my childhood it was Sivia who taught me all of the paratactic details which were necessary to live what she called "the good life." I was a quick study. No sooner had Sivia mentioned a new rule than I was already following it.

There was a
               lariat in the house that belonged to Sivia's father, and it was made of gold. Whenever Sivia put that magic lariat around someone, it made that person do Sivia's bidding. I was curious to know how it worked but Sivia said you couldn't explain magical things, they just were. I watched Sivia use the magic lariat on storekeepers and salespeople and even once on a doctor of veterinary medicine who refused to treat her iguana. Sivia never had to use the magic lariat on me, of course, because I always did what she told me anyway.

There was a house
                    across from ours where our enemies lived. Actually they were first Sivia's enemies, and then Plastic Man's enemies, and then they became my enemies too. Plastic Man was Sivia's grandson and he was my grandfather.

[8]

They were the only people I lived with. The rest of our family had died or had been sent away by Sivia for disobeying her. My own father, Sivia's great-grandson, Plastic Man's son, was sent away from Appearance House on the day after the day I was born. There was some disagreement about what I was to be named and for some reason Sivia's magic lariat would not work on my father. So she banished him. My mother, who had been a Princess in the Land of Porcelain, died the day I was born. She is buried in the yard behind Appearance House, near Plastic Man's garden.

The house where our enemies lived was called Transparent House and it was made of glass. There was nothing in there that was not made of glass except for the people, a father and his little boy who was named Christopher. Sivia would look from our window and observe everything that went on across the street and she would shudder aloud.

When I got old enough she would let me look at the ugly things that went on in Transparent House so I would know how lucky I was to be living with her and Plastic Man in Appearance House. Our life was so tidy that our plates were taken away after every bite we ate and they were cleaned before we got them back to us for the next bite. It was a long time before I learned about things like crumbs and dust.

There was a house. I
        once behaved badly and sneaked across the street to it while Sivia was making apple jelly and Plastic Man was sleeping on the floor. I walked into the house but all that transparency frightened me so much I had to leave right away. There was no one in the house, that was easy to tell, but in the backyard I saw the boy named Christopher playing with himself and a few insects.

"Hey, you can't do that," I told him.

"Mind your own business," he said.

[9]

"It's not nice."

Then Christopher said an unheard-of word.

I went over to him, very frustrated and angry, but before I could tell him what Sivia might do to him he punched me right in my right eye with what must have been all his might.

I was startled. The first thing I thought of when it happened was how the expression Plastic Man once used when he fell over Sivia's iguana, "I could see stars," was true. The stars I saw were kind of pink and pastel and exploding things. But I knew I couldn't let Christopher's action go unpunished, especially in the yard behind Transparent House, where any- one could see it. So I punched Christopher in his right eye with all my might. Or with what I thought was all my might. It seemed to work.

Then he punched me in my left eye.

Then I punched him in *his* left eye.

All four of our eyes were swollen shut in a few minutes and neither of us could see anything, so we sort of had to feel our way back to our own houses.

There was a house. I was told by Sivia when I got home that I had done a bad thing. Plastic Man just laughed, but she sent him up to his room for that, and after that he stopped.

Sivia went to the room that had belonged to my late mother, the Princess from the Land of Porcelain, and she got out a pair of sunglasses that had very dark lenses and she put them on me so no one could see how discolored and swollen my eyes were.

After dinner Christopher and his father came over and his father looked very angry.

"I don't allow angry people in Appearance House," Sivia told Christopher's father at the door. So they stayed outside.

"Your son gave my son two black eyes," Christopher's father said. I was watching from the spiral staircase. Christopher wasn't wearing any sunglasses. His eyes were black and swollen shut.

"I have no son," Sivia told the man.

"Your grandson, then," he shot back.

"Look at my grandson over there," she said, pointing to Plastic Man, who was all curled up like a snake in the looking-room. "He's too peaceful to hurt anyone."

"I mean that boy by the steps!" Christopher's father yelled, pointing to me. I ran up a few steps, out of his sight.

"That's my great-great-grandson."

"Whoever he is . . . . He could have blinded my son. I demand that you punish him."

Sivia looked almost angry. "I will, but only for disobeying me and going across the street, not for hitting anyone from a transparent house. He's a moral boy and he can't help what he does outside our home."

And Sivia slammed the door.

There was a house. I was a
                                good boy after that. Even after a
week, when my eyes cleared up, I still kept wearing my sunglasses. This pleased Sivia. Plastic Man said he liked it too although Plastic Man was content with just about anything that happened in Appearance House just so long as he could turn into a snake or a pie or a vitamin pill. Once I asked him where he got his powers and he told me he got them from his position and that I would understand someday. He told me this while he was a kitchen table.

I liked my dark glasses because they were the only thing I had of my parents'. Sivia had locked the room in which the Princess and my father had slept, and there was no way she would tell me my father's name. I asked Plastic Man but he said he had forgotten it.

There was a house. I was a boy
who was curious about certain
things like the density of the planet Mercury and the number
of toads in the Amazon and the chemical composition of
various household appliances. I had strange habits. I ate
tissues. Sivia thought this was my way of telling her I was
unhappy so she set about to make me happy.

"There's nothing wrong with you," she told me as she
put her magic lariat around me.

"You are happy," Sivia told me, her golden lariat grip-
ping me tightly.

"I am happy," I repeated. "There's nothing wrong with
me." After that I only wore my sunglasses in the house. Outside I took them off.

There was a house. I was a boy there.
When Sivia would take
me for walks, she would always hold me by the hand. She
said this was because she was so used to the refined air of
Appearance House that the polluted air of outside made her
dizzy. But I figured she just wanted to be as close as possible
to me and play our game.

Our game was this: Whenever we would come across a
person who we thought was bad, one of us would squeeze the
other's hand. Usually bad people came in pairs. Sometimes
they held hands. Once I wondered aloud whether those
people might be playing the same game and squeezing each
other's hand when they saw Sivia and me walking down the
street. She laughed and said no, how could anyone else have
learned about our game? It didn't seem very likely.

There was a house. I was a boy there. I

had problems with
my arteries because they weren't getting enough blood from
my heart because they were too filled with other things. This
made me weak, too weak to read my books or see plays with
Sivia or help Plastic Man with his marigolds. So they reluc-
tantly decided to take me to the hospital and let me stay
there for a month till I was better. I didn't care so long as I
would feel better. Sivia didn't like the idea of my sleeping
outside Appearance House, but I promised her I'd save up all
my sleeping time until I got home.

One night, just after I had settled into the hospital and
was feeling like I had more blood, a candy-striper crept into
my bed. She was blonde, blonder than I, and she was a deaf-
mute. She didn't understand when I told her what she was
doing was crazy. I was still too weak to punch her in the eye
as I had done with Christopher. So the blonde candy-striper
poked me, licked me, slipped into me, panted and danced
over me, grew happier than I had ever imagined people were
meant to be. Finally it was over and she kissed me behind the
ear, a wet kiss, and she slithered out of my hospital bed.

In the morning it took me a long time to figure out why
it was raining indoors.

There was a house. I was a boy there. I had
no patience after
that for staying in the hospital. My arteries had swelled up
and all the garbage in them had gone away, so Plastic Man
came by and picked me up and took me back to Appearance
House where Sivia was waiting. She was painting the tombstones in back of the house. Sivia asked me if I was well
enough to help her and I said yes, so she let me paint my
mother's tombstone orange. She painted her father's tombstone forest green.

"My father was the saintliest man that ever lived," Sivia

[13]

told me. Plastic Man gave a snort from the kitchen but Sivia ignored him.

There was a house. I was a boy there. I had to

catch up on
all my sleep for Sivia's sake. I didn't want her to know that I'd lied to her and actually slept in the hospital. Sivia had me sleep for five days straight after we finished painting the tombstones. She took photographs of my dreams. On the fifth day Sivia woke me up by slapping me because I had a terrible dream. In the dream an old man was having sex with my mother, the Princess from the Land of Porcelain. I knew it had something to do with me, their having sex.

"It was just a dream," Sivia said as she shook me awake. "I am your great-great-grandmother and nothing more. My father was a saint. I am not your half-sister, believe me."

First I was groggy and didn't know what she was talking about but then I remembered the tombstones.

There was a house. I was a boy there. I had to leave.

I left two days after my seventeenth birthday. Appearance House had rapidly decayed after my dream. Plastic Man was missing and we never could find him. Sivia thought he might have swallowed the bone of a boiled white cat and made himself invisible. Sivia knew I was leaving. She knew her golden lariat wouldn't work on me because I knew the secret, the same secret that her own son, the husband of the Princess from the Land of Porcelain, had found out. Sivia was finally beginning to look her age when I left. "I'll be back to visit," I told her. "No, you won't" was what she said to me. Sivia was right.

FOR THE TIME BEING

They do it with mirrors.

That is how other people live. They have tricks I do not know about. My education has been inadequate. No one ever taught me how to live.

When I was fifteen months old, just after they took me on the merry-go-round for the first time, I began making strange faces in my crib. To my mother it appeared that a terrible struggle was going on inside of me. She called my father home from work in the middle of the day. They took me to the pediatrician. He put me on tranquilizers. I was fifteen months old. Still the faces continued. My mother blamed it on the merry-go-round.

I am now twenty-five years old, a practicing attorney, a notary public, a divorced man. I am one-eighth the age of the country I live in. And I still make faces. Also, I talk to myself. I am a good listener.

I had what I call a nervous breakdown after I passed the bar exams, after my wife left me to live with her lover, another woman. I am all right now. I work for a firm on Wall Street. I handle municipal bonds. There are less interesting things to do.

When I was fourteen, I began a collection of autographed covers of *Time* magazine. It was a big deal then to get your face on the cover of *Time* magazine. I always fantasized about the day that my face would appear on the cover of *Time* magazine. Now I am pretty sure that will never happen. I am one-eighth the age of my nation; according to the Constitution, I should be in Congress already. And I do not even have a girlfriend. I am still in love with my ex-wife.

Maura will not write me. She lives in Chicago now, with Vivian, her lover. I have never met Vivian, but I bear her no ill will. After all, she only ruined my life, and in the long run we are all dead anyway, so it does not matter. Vivian should live and be well. That is what my grandmother would have said. Maura should live and be well, too. I hope she is happy. I hope she gives me a second thought now and then. More than that I have no right to ask.

When I was fourteen, I wrote letters like this:

"Dear Bishop Pike,

"I am a fourteen-year-old boy who collects autographed *Time* magazine covers. I hope you will autograph the enclosed cover and return it to me. I have always admired you and liked your book *If This Be Hearsay* and the others, too."

Then I would say thank you and sincerely sign my name. It was my first form letter. The first two sentences were always the same. The last sentence I changed for each person. What I wrote was always a compliment. Today in my law office there is a machine called MTST which does the same thing automatically. Every person thinks he is getting a personal reply, when all it is, *is* a form letter with something personal in it.

I got autographed *Time* magazine covers from everyone. Barbra Streisand signed, "Happy days always." Governor Scranton of Pennsylvania sent me an autographed photo which he said was better than the magazine cover. Martin Luther King used a stamp; or rather, the person who stamped the magazine cover "Martin Luther King" used a stamp. Most

[16]

of the signatures seemed real.

At first I could not believe it. It was so easy. All these famous people, senators, corporation executives, actors, racing-car drivers, Latin American dictators, were all sending me their signatures on my own magazine cover. With my name stuck on the white subscription label on the bottom. Finally it got too easy, and then *Time* magazine started putting abstract designs on their cover instead of portraits of people, and then I gave up. My last cover was Chief Justice Burger. I quit after that.

To this day I have over 150 autographed *Time* magazine covers somewhere in my mother's house. Or perhaps she has sold them at auction. Walter Cronkite wrote, "To a fine young man . . . ." If Walter Cronkite said it, it must have been true. So that's the way it was: I was a fine young man. I didn't know that until Walter Cronkite told me. How did he know?

Richard Nixon and Lyndon Johnson signed with an Autopen. That is a device that signs signatures to make them look like they are real. I knew all along that it was a machine. No President has ever fooled me. Parents, friends, my wife— they have all fooled me. But never have I been fooled by my President.

I remember buying a particular *Time* magazine. This was before I had a subscription. I went on the Utica Avenue bus to Church Avenue, bought the magazine at the newsstand. On the cover were the astronauts McDivitt and White. They flew Gemini Something. White was the first American to walk in space. Later he was killed in the Apollo fire. I bought the magazine with McDivitt and White on it, and then I realized that I only had a nickel left. Bus fare was fifteen cents. At least if I had a dime I could call my mother. Church and Utica was far from my house. It was beginning to get dark. My mother was expecting me. I decided to walk home.

It took me an hour to walk home. I did not mind. In fact, I was rather glad to be alone on a journey. I passed the post office and the bank that had been robbed the month before and Dan Lurie's barbell store, which featured an enormous picture of Dan Lurie and all of his muscles. I was very skinny. But that didn't matter. I had my *Time* magazine.

The hallmark of my life has always been self-indulgence. I see that now. When what's-her-name left me, I really didn't mind. I actually enjoyed it. It was the first time I had ever lived alone. Yet for some reason I broke down. Maybe it was the drinking water. Who knows? I never learned how to live properly. Four years of college, three years of law school, and I still don't have the slightest idea of how living is done. You would think that I should have picked it up somewhere along the way: on Utica Avenue, perhaps, or from one of my *Time* magazine cover friends.

Bishop Pike signed his name very small. His son committed suicide on my birthday ten years ago. The boy was confused and taking Romilar and acid and lonely in a New York hotel room. He shouldn't have done it. I never did. A few years after that, there was a seance on Canadian television and Bishop Pike's son told his father that he regretted the suicide. It all means nothing to me.

Yes. I indulge myself too much. I apologize. If only I were a fictional character, then I could excuse myself for being the product of a self-indulgent writer. But I'm real, I swear it. The "I" of this story is really me, Richard Grayson, and not some literary device. You can call this fiction if you want to, but it is true. I know I am still not well. I am typing this now and it makes no sense and then I will go to the Junction and have it Xeroxed at the Quick Copy Center and then I will collate my copies and then I will put them in a

manila envelope and send them out to little magazines and
little magazine editors will look at this and send it right back
to me with a clever little rejection notice. Well, that is how
life is. That is how my life is. I never learned how to live
properly, and damn it, that's not my fault. I don't place the
blame on you, but if you're an editor reading this and you
don't publish it, I hope your conscience is clear. One more
rejection and I could do what Bishop Pike's son did. And
then you'll be sorry. I don't care if you do think I'm crazy. I
don't care if I've completely lost control of this story. I'm
not going to stop here. Look. I've had it up to here with
rejections. I can't take any more. Suicide in my age bracket
is becoming more common. My brother's friend jumped off
a building last spring: you can read about it in another of my
stories. Of course, that one didn't get published either. One
of these days somebody is going to have my death on their
conscience. And years from now, they'll be on Canadian television at some seance and I'll come back and tell them that
they killed me as surely as I killed off the stupid narrator of
this story and his fucking *Time* magazine covers. I'm sick of
making up characters anyway. I don't even like to fucking
write. It's just that I'm not much good for anything else.
Please: you can see I'm a sick person. What would it take, a
few pages in your lousy literary magazine, to make me happy?
I work hard on my stories and yet I seem to be getting
nowhere. Will you put this in print, *please*, minus this last
paragraph? The last line of this story should be, "It all means
nothing to me." You've got to do it. I'm so miserable. I
want to die. Sometimes I really wish I *had* gone to law school
and been married and collected *Time* magazine covers. Oh
God. I'm so lonely. I'm sorry about this, about spilling my
guts out to you here, but my life hasn't been very good. Yes,
God damn it, I want your sympathy! If I can't have your
respect, I'll settle for your pity . . . for the time being, at

least.

How do other people manage to get through life? This is not a rhetorical question.

A HARD WOMAN

Something Naomi will never forgive herself for

She was forty-five years old. Her father-in-law had had a heart attack two months before. Naomi and David were visiting his parents in Florida. David's father had retired the year before, when their pants business had gone under after fifty years. David had worked with his father his whole adult life. It was hard for him to act on his own. David had taken a partner, a refugee old enough to be his father, and they were importing jeans from Taiwan. Naomi hated the partner, called him *the mocky*, wanted David to break up with him and go into business with Vince Fabrizio in Florida. She told her father-in-law all these things as they walked.

Naomi had never liked David's mother or his sister. She had started going out with David when he was eighteen and she was thirteen, and David's mother and sister persisted in treating her like a child, a selfish child. But her father-in-law had always been good to her. She had named her third daughter Natalie after her father-in-law's father Nathan. Her father-in-law was a generous man, a very hard worker. When she would look at photos of him she would laugh and say that he always looked like a Mafiosi in photos because of his small

[21]

stature and tinted eyeglasses and big cigar tilted downwards. He looked like a Mafiosi as they walked together along the outskirts of the condominium that Sunday morning. Her father-in-law was eighty years old.

"I don't know what it is, Naomi," he told her, "but I just miss Davey so much."

She imagined herself smiling at this. Inside she was wondering if her father-in-law would start crying on the way to the airport as he had the time before, when they had come down to see him through the heart attack. She dreaded the thought of seeing her father-in-law cry. David was fifty years old.

Before she knew what was happening, her father-in-law's arms were around her shoulders. "I love you," he was telling her. "I *love* you," he said to Naomi.

She was embarrassed by this.

Two weeks later Naomi's father-in-law would go bait in a pinochle game and be so disgusted with himself that he would bring on another heart attack. They revived him with oxygen in the card room, but it took too long. The five minutes without oxygen did too much damage to his brain. The next time Naomi saw her father-in-law, he was not, as the doctors told them, "a viable, functioning being." He was a vegetable connected to machines.

Two days before the funeral Naomi told her oldest daughter Elise what she would never forgive herself for. Naomi cried.

"But Mom," Elise told Naomi. "He *knew*."

Naomi was still crying. "But why couldn't I say it? It was the truth . . . ."

This was the third time Elise could remember seeing Naomi cry.

Something Naomi wants

"What do you want, Mom?" Elise asked Naomi. Elise was twenty-five years old, twenty years younger than Naomi.

Naomi was coming out of the bathroom. She was wearing her housedress with a bathing suit underneath. Earlier she and David had been in the pool.

"Some more diet soda in the refrigerator," Naomi told her daughter. "Seven-Up."

"What do you want?" Elise asked as she put some cans in the refrigerator.

"You've got to wash those cans first," Naomi said.

Naomi and Elise began rinsing off the soda cans. They were putting them in the refrigerator when her daughter asked her a third time.

"No, I mean *what do you want?*"

Naomi started to sing. "All I want is a room somewhere . . . " in a Cockney accent.

"What do you want?"

"Health for my family."

"No, for yourself alone. What do you want?"

"My husband." David was upstairs watching Jimmy Connors and Bjorn Borg.

"You *have* him. Something you don't have." Elise was in one of her moods.

"Nothing," she told her daughter. She was cleaning the kitchen counter.

"Nothing?"

"Nothing."

"Are you sure?"

Natalie, her youngest daughter, had heard all this. She came into the room. "This is going to end up in a fight, Elise, so why don't you leave her alone?"

"Oh go to hell," Elise told Natalie. Naomi went on with her cleaning. Elise stormed out of the room. Natalie smirked, took a can of diet soda out of the refrigerator, sat down at the table. She was fifteen years old. Naomi had been thirty when Natalie was born.

Something Naomi has underlined in a book

Elise was so depressed about being twenty-five and divorced and living in her parents' house again that she got under the covers at three o'clock in the afternoon. She wanted to die.

After an hour of wanting to die, she remembered a book she had once read, *Do-It-Yourself Psychotherapy*. She found the book in Natalie's room. Natalie made some stupid remark, but Elise just ignored her. While their parents were in Florida, Elise mostly ignored her.

Elise read a few chapters and felt well enough to broil herself a hamburger for dinner. She was leafing through the book when she saw a passage that was underlined. It was in the chapter called "Parents." The passage was this:

So there are no suggestions I have to offer you as a parent, except to bear in mind that whatever you do, it is likely to be wrong in your child's eyes. But when and if your child grows to maturity—if he or she doesn't get stuck in childlike or adolescent behavior—your child will come to appreciate that you did the best you could.

Elise shook her head. She knew it was Naomi who did the underlining, and she knew her mother meant for her to pick it up one day, as she did.

Something Naomi says when people take advantage of her

"You're not going to get away with this, you know."

Something Naomi remembers

When Naomi's brother was born, she was five years old. Her mother lost a great deal of blood from the hemorrhaging, and she tried to strangle a doctor with his tie. After that they had no choice but to commit Naomi's mother to the state hospital. She was there five months. Naomi lived with her father and her father's parents. She loved her grandmother because she was soft and round and smelled of flour. Her grandfather scared her at first, because he would say *"Gay in dred!"* back to her grandmother, and the old man would laugh. Naomi's father looked tired a lot of the time.

One day her grandmother dressed her in a dress. Her father took her on the bus and they went to the state hospital. They waited in a room with bare walls and finally a nurse brought Naomi's mother in.

Her mother screamed when she saw Naomi.

Naomi started crying. She had never been so scared of another person before. Her mother kept screaming until they had to take her away.

All her life Naomi would never forget the scream. When she was fifty-five and her mother was seventy-five and a perfectly normal old woman living by the boardwalk and playing cards and doing volunteer work as a foster grandparent, Naomi still would not be able to forget her mother's screams.

Something a young man in Boulder, Colorado, says about Naomi

Chris walked in the apartment and found Patti in the bathroom crying. Patti was Naomi's middle daughter. She was twenty-three years old.

"What's the matter, Pat?"

Patti said nothing, turned on the faucet so she could drown out Chris' questions and her own sobs.

Chris pounded on the door for a while. Then he said, "What the hell," and got out a beer.

Eventually Patti came out of the bathroom. "I thought we'd have zucchini and mushrooms tonight," she said.

Chris didn't look up from his book. He said, "Fine."

Two nights later Chris found the letter from Naomi while he was looking for a postage stamp in Patti's desk. He read the letter quickly because he was afraid Patti would come in the room at any time. By the time Chris read the sentence, *Why don't you just forget I'm your mother?*, he realized why Patti had been crying two days before.

Chris will never say anything to Patti about Naomi's letter. To Willachek, his friend at the bookstore, he will say, "Patti's mother, boy, she's a real *hard woman*."

Willachek will nod and think, *No wonder Pat's so messed up, with a mother like that.* Then he and Chris will change the subject. There is no sense in having a conversation about someone like Naomi.

ROOMINATIONS

Call me 096-46-6557.

"What are you feeling?" my fiancee asks me.
"Feelinglessness," I reply.

My fiancee and I are moving to a large city in Canada, in the province most likely to secede. There we will not be numbers but people.

"Some orgasms are better than others," I tell my fiancee.
"So what?" she says.

We have lunch with Frederick, who is to be my best man.
"Who cares if I'm celibate?" Frederick says, "I don't give a fuck."
My fiancee drinks her liqueur and says, "There is no such thing as neuroses anymore. What we all suffer from are *socioses*."
Frederick and I nod, more out of laziness than agreement.

Unbeknownst to myself, my fiancee is not human at all, but a creature from another galaxy—the planet Flaubert, to be exact.

Cowards run in my family. Nevertheless I show up for my wedding. Frederick is our only witness. My wife's son by a previous marriage is taking his medical school exams. I manage not to faint during the ceremony. It is, as they say, virtually painless.

My wife and I stand in a cemetery in front of the grave of the woman in whose womb I lived for forty-one weeks. Neither of us says anything; we are on our honeymoon.

We settle in our model home. All of the rooms are roped off so we cannot go in them and mess them up. We must live in hallways and foyers and lobbies and vestibules from now on.

My wife is smiling at me, asking me to come to her.
I look at her body and think: Surely there is nothing less sexy than a somebody naked.

We pass a dead body on the subway tracks. Police and television reporters are hovering over it. We don't really know if it makes us feel bad. Mostly it seems like re-seeing a scene in a movie whose title we can't recall.

I have a masters and my wife has a johnson, but still we have problems. My wife tells me that my trouble is I expect her to have a *grand mal* seizure every night.

I used to feel guilty about having sex. Now I feel guilty about *not* having it.

"Why don't you do something with your life?" my wife

asks me.

"It's all this free time," I complain. "How can anybody be expected to accomplish anything with all this free time?"

We pass a group of television reporters covering a group of television reporters covering a group of television reporters.

"Look at that," my wife points. "There's nobody at the center of things."

My wife's son from a previous marriage comes to visit us. He sleeps in our downstairs foyer. He is an Orthodox Jewish medical student. Because of some obscure Talmudic principle, he tells us, he can only dissect Orthodox Jewish cadavers.

With my wife occupied with her son, I can go out to a bar and at eleven o'clock I can say, "At this time of night I'm usually in bed . . . alone."

A woman says, "There, there," and pats my ankle twice, one time for each "there."

I ask my stepson if he ever takes risks and he answers, "Yes. Sometimes. Calculated ones." My stepson is a great admirer of the late Clifton Webb.

Neither my wife nor my stepson nor I can get out of bed in the morning. I cry when I miss a traffic light. My wife cannot stop crying after nicking her calf with a razor. My stepson is unable to help us because he is comatose. That Tolstoyan moment my professors used to speak of will never arrive.

My wife's father, an obese mathematician, arrives to tend to us. Looking at my father-in-law makes me want never to do another quadratic equation again. But he gets us all back in shape. Meanwhile he cleans out my refrigerator. He eats meatball after meatball in front of our noses, toothpicks and all.

My father-in-law is missing. My stepson and I look in the parking lot near the computer, but there is no sign of him. The only sign says: For Employees Only. And then we remember that there is no way we can find my father-in-law because he is dead.

People around us are aging quickly. Mustaches are falling off. Hair turns grey. Skin gets leathery. My stepson's friend from medical school, Jiro Kindo, comes to stay with us. He pronounces *leathery* "rezary."

Now that the dog days are over, now that those serious, sweaty, skinful days of summer are gone, the Spanish Blue days have arrived. My wife dreads the Spanish Blue days. She hates the smell of fish.

We lie in bed, over the covers not under them. Our freshly blow-dried hair fluffs out over our pillows. Our minds whirr. Our fists are curled up. Her mouth is half-open. My penis is half-erect.

There are demi-dreams, quivers. Occasionally we forget, and we are back in the cemetery in the ninety-degree sun, blistering our feet on our parents' graves.

I take the subway in the morning: trains that are too new and too empty. When there are not enough people, the air conditioning is too strong, and I must stop my eyes from closing, my head from falling on the orange shoulder of the science-fiction-reading woman next to me, a woman who is not my wife.

My stepson never says, "*Je m'en fiche*," but Jiro Kindo
does. I like having him around. He is useless and irrelevant
and mostly superfluous, but he makes our house a good place
to hibernate.

When Jiro Kindo gets in his car, the buzzer does not buzz
even though he does not buckle his seat-belt. He has no
weight, no mass, no avoirdupois or corduroy. He looks at my
stepson with love. My stepson has a cleft in his chin, and his
jeans are cut off, and the hairs on his legs are more blond than
brown. My stepson's yarmulke is sewed onto his head. My
stepson carries the book *Stranger in a Strange Land* and gives
it as a gift to Jiro Kindo, who does not grok anything yet.

My wife is so worried about her son that she will not go
to the bathroom. I think of the old days when we were only
engaged. In those days I could not get her *out* of the bathroom.

One night my wife is finally awakened. She goes to an
auction at the edge of the sea and she takes off her night
brace. I follow her and tell her that the orthodontist has
warned her she must wear it all the time. She will wear it only
sporadically and grudgingly because she fears it is causing her
asthma. She may be right. I do not know.

I put the golf clubs in the trunk of Jiro Kindo's car. The
Tang from Houston goes in the back seat. My stepson is ready
to drive Jiro Kindo into the waiting arms of the grinning Sky-
cap by the KLM terminal.

My stepson kisses Jiro Kindo on the lips. "Farewell,"

[31]

he says. "You will make errors of judgment, undoubtedly, but soon it will all be far away."

My wife sighs. "Jiro Kindo is gone," she says. "The Tylenol years have ended at last. We have survived it yet."

But sooner than we can imagine, Jiro Kindo is on television. He is holding three girls in powder blue Danskins hostage. They are scared he will shoot them. My wife and I watch as Jiro Kindo demands, quietly but determinedly, safe passage to our room.

My wife is against it, but I am human, so I call and try to make the proper arrangements. There is no time and the phone lines are all down and the cardinal in our willow tree is no carrier pigeon. So Jiro Kindo is killed, shot thirty-three times by the Malaysian police. My stepson comes home crying. He recites Kaddish.

My wife leaves our home and wanders into Beirut. She tries to relax and use the Nikon that Jiro Kindo left behind. When she tries to photograph the fruits in the marketplace, men come over and grab her. At first she thinks it is I and her son. But they put her into a Beirut jail and they slap her and grill her and have Lebanese babies cheese up on her and they demand her diplomatic pouch. When she does not produce one, she is shot seventy-four times in the abdomen.

Back in my room there is red sobbing in the simultaneous dawn. My wife was an annual in a garden of perennials. She was just a child herself, like her father, like her son, like me. Without her, life will be a tolerable drag, but nothing more.

When he is finished reciting Kaddish, my stepson looks

at me. We are in the upstairs hallway.

"What are you feeling?" he asks me.

I stare at the back of his head, at his yarmulke.

"What are you feeling?" he asks again.

I close my eyes. "Self-indulgence," I tell him. "There is no end to it."

And my stepson says another prayer.

NOTHING WRONG WITH THE MACHINERY

What's your objective?

She stared at Kevin's letter.

What's your objective?

She thought of him walking out of the optometrist's office with his new soft contact lenses. Of him looking at his reflection in every store window on Avenue U. Of him bursting to tell the older woman who took his order, one Quarter Pounder, regular fries, small Coke, at the McDonald's. Of him tearing and seeing the children crossing the street so blurry.

What's your objective?

He always asked her questions like that. One night in the Rosebud Cafe on Main Street in Middlebury, Vermont 05753 upstairs at a varnished table eating Bulgar pilaf and drinking red zinger tea with honey, he pushed his glasses up his nose with his finger and asked her

What's your objective?

She laughed. He asked her again.

What's your objective?

and she asked him what his was, a question for a question, imitating psychiatry, the Jewish science.

What's your objective?

"Easy," Kevin said. "I want someone who'll make me forget all the lovers that I never had." And he sipped his tea and his glasses fell down his nose again.

And now he would write her letters, letters to all the places she moved to without telling him and each time the same question —

What's your objective?

Finally she just stopped reading the letters. The handwriting on the envelopes got smaller and smaller as the months went on and finally the letters stopped.

What's your objective?

She put on a Billie Holliday record of her mother's and dabbed Noxzema on her face. Next to her was her childhood doll, Pinky, her leg torn off. The pillows were fuzzy. The music made her close her eyes.

When her television set broke, she didn't mind at first.

But then someone at school told her of a really first-rate BBC serial on *Masterpiece Theatre*, so she called a repairman. She picked him out by name in the Yellow Pages: Pyramid TV Repair. Pyramids had energy.

The repairman was young, taller than Kevin, more shy. The same curly blond hair.

What's your objective? she wanted to ask him.

But instead she asked: "Why won't it play?"

He kept looking inside the set for a proper answer. Finally he said apologetically: "There's nothing wrong with the machinery, far as I can tell."

This was too much. "What?" she said stupidly.

"The parts are all there," the repairman said. "Nothing is broken. Sometimes it gets like that—they just won't go."

What's your objective?

"Something needs fixing," she told him. "It won't play."

The repairman grinned. He didn't wear glasses. "Give her time, she'll come round."

She couldn't say anything. She was wearing a University

[35]

of Wisconsin tee shirt and he was staring at both *i*'s.

"You don't have to pay me or anything." He started to take out a cigarette. It was a joint. She must have looked startled or disapproving or unfriendly because he left without offering her a toke. Or saying goodbye.

Two mornings later she got *Captain Kangaroo*. It was fuzzy and the colors were all wrong but she could make out the action. She remembered how Kevin said the only imitation he could do was Mister Moose.

Good morning, Captain. What's your objective?

She was doing a paper for semantics called *The Contradiction Factor*. She was in the library looking up old journal articles she could use. Somebody brushed by her and she was sure it was Kevin for the minute. But this person had glasses on and Kevin didn't wear his anymore.

Then she smelled lilacs from her great-uncle's garden and she knew she needed more sleep. Still, the paper was due in two days and she needed more sources. As it was she'd have to spend a whole night typing it up.

In a back number of the journal *Etc.* she found an article she needed. It was by S.I. Hayakawa. She read the first paragraph.

"There's nothing wrong with the machinery. The parts are all there. Nothing is broken. But sometimes it just won't go."

What machinery?

She closed the journal and something in her stomach tightened. Somewhere around her navel. The solar plexus. Kevin called her navel "Willie" for some reason.

She ran out of the library, forgetting her coat. When she got home she took a valium and turned on the television. She got a deliciously familiar soap opera. Nancy Hughes was still in her kitchen so everything was all right.

She cracked her neck a few times, took yogic "cleansing breaths." The colors on the set were better. Nancy Hughes was talking to her husband Chris about the new woman in Oakdale. Chris was defending the woman. Nancy asked him how he could be so sure the new woman was all right. "After all, we don't know her objectives," Nancy said.

She shut off the television set and scrambled for her phone book. Nancy and Chris Hughes were fading out. She was looking frantically for Kevin's phone number. She misdialed at first and got a Chinese laundry. Then she used the right area code and heard the familiar ringing of Kevin's plain black telephone. She could hardly wait for him to ask her the question again.

It took five rings. "Hello," Kevin finally said. He sounded out of breath. He was six states away from her.

She hung up quickly. He wouldn't have asked her her objective. They would have had to talk of trivial things, of school, of parents, of politics. She didn't want to talk about those things anymore.

Now she only wanted to answer the question.

A SENSE OF PORPOISE

Yes. Of course, you're right. My life has changed drastically since the porpoise came to live with me. Before he arrived, I experienced life in only three flavors: spearmint, peppermint, and disappointment. Now things have opened up a little.

At first I thought he was a dolphin. What did I know then? But no, he told me. "Look at me," he said, "my nose is blunt, unlike a dolphin's." Then he sighed, a sigh I have since become used to hearing. "Only in America are porpoises mistaken for dolphins."

The first thing he did was to arrange for a production of Thornton Wilder's "Our Town" to be held at a neighborhood church. The porpoise directed the play and he himself played the role of the Stage Manager. It was incredible, all those people and he, acting for an audience of just one: me. They performed the play over and over again for six successive nights, until I finally broke down and cried at the end, as my father used to. How did the porpoise know that the ending of "Our Town" was the only thing my father ever cried at? And why was he going to all this trouble just for me? I couldn't understand it.

"Who sent you here?" I would shout at him, losing my temper in my usual mock-ferocious way. He would just go on with his business, dusting the furniture with Pledge or watching a hockey game on television. "I'll answer you when you've calmed down and can talk like a civilized human being," he would tell me calmly.

This endless patience of his exasperated me. Yet somehow I never could bring myself to ask him to leave. Down deep, I knew it: I was in trouble with my life and needed the porpoise's help. But I didn't have to let him know how much I appreciated his presence. So I would taunt him about being so out of his element, those waters of the North Atlantic and North Pacific. "You look like a fish, but you're not a fish," I would chant in my worst little-boy whine. Or I would call him an Oreo, referring to his white underside in the middle of an otherwise black body. But he just sat there, sipping his iced tea and reading the *Christian Science Monitor.*

"Do I remind you of your father?" he asked me one day.

I snorted. "Well, you were both mammals, but the resemblance ends there."

The porpoise gave me one of his sighs again.

"Yes," I gave in. "You do, a little. You know my father was a psychiatrist, a strict Freudian?"

The porpoise nodded.

"One day, when I was seven or eight," I told him, my eyes closing with embarrassment, "I found my father's telephone book in his office. He used the den of our house as an office. I looked up the names of his patients and I called them all up, telling them that my father had just died and they needn't come in for their next appointment."

The porpoise chuckled softly. "And what was your father's reaction?"

"He sent me to another psychiatrist. And all I wanted was *him*. I was so sick of competing with his patients. They told such interesting stories, they kept my father spellbound . . . . How could I, a little boy, compete with that?"

[39]

"So you killed him off in your fantasies," the porpoise said. "And that served him right, huh?"

"Please, I don't want to talk about it anymore."

The porpoise took a sip of iced tea. "And when your father really died, how was it then?"

I said nothing and went into the kitchen, but the porpoise was there before I was, already preparing a meat loaf dinner.

It was then that I realized he was with me for good. And it was only a day later that I realized that I couldn't live without him.

On Saturday evenings, the porpoise arranged an hour of joke-telling. We would each tell each other stories and try to make the other one laugh. It was a sort of contest. The porpoise naturally always won. He was straight-faced at the funniest jokes, claiming he'd heard them before or that I was telling them all wrong. Then he'd tell a stupid joke and I'd laugh like hell. I don't know; maybe it was just his appearance that I was laughing at.

"Did you know that Iranians can telephone each other Persian to Persian?" he'd quip, and I'd crack up completely.

Or he would tell me another joke and while I was doubled up with laughter, he'd say, "So that was funny enough for you, eh, my mutant prince?" And the pains in my stomach would just get that much worse.

Try as I would, I could never manage to get a smile out of that snubbed snout of his.

One Saturday night, after the alarm clock rang, signalling the end of our joke-telling hour, I asked the porpoise just what he was doing with me.

"I've read up on the subject," I told him, "and I know you porpoises are sociable animals. Sometimes you travel in groups of more than a hundred. Don't you miss the company of other porpoises? Don't you miss the ocean? Why have you

[40]

come here to bother with me at all?" I stopped all laughing and began crying quite softly and rhythmically. "Why me?" I sobbed. "I'm nobody."

For the first time I could remember, he actually tried to touch me. But he couldn't quite get his flipper to make contact with my shoulder.

"I'm nobody," I repeated, my face in my hands.

"Ah," he said to me, "but now you're a porpoise's nobody."

We took a trip together down to the mountains. He did most of the driving. We were making our way along a deserted country road one night when I awoke in the back seat and heard the radio playing "The Way We Were." Then after Barbra Streisand stopped singing, I heard the announcer say the weather in Montreal was unseasonably mild.

"Are we in Montreal?" I jumped up and demanded of the porpoise. For a second I actually thought he was kidnapping me.

My outburst must have startled him, for he lost control of the wheel for a mini-moment, and the car swerved a little. Luckily there were no other cars about.

"Hush," the porpoise said to me. I looked at his snout in the rear-view mirror. "At night you can pick up faraway radio stations." He moved around the dial and it was true. We were getting Dallas, Charleston, Denver.

"Have a little faith," the porpoise said.

I fell asleep again and dreamed of my father. In the morning the porpoise took me to a Howard Johnson's for pancakes.

We had a marvelous vacation, camping out, hiking, climbing the slopes, fishing. Of course the porpoise was more adept at fishing than I, being used to preying on small fishes as he was. I asked him if he thought there was something wrong in that.

[41]

The porpoise's snout flared a little. "No," he said. "I don't think so. It's only natural. Take my mother, for instance ... "

He had never before spoken of any relative, much less mentioned his mother, so I listened intently.

"Her natural state was to be a mother, to mother one child at a time. She never thought about whether it was right or ecologically feasible or destructive to be a mother; she just did it. Do you know that she nursed me as we swam through the waters?"

I said nothing. He had never revealed this much of himself before, and in a way I was touched that he felt free enough with me to share what was so obviously intimate a memory. So that time I touched him. The lubricating oil on his black body felt sticky to the touch, and I admit I was a bit queasy for a moment, especially after I remembered reading that certain Eskimo tribes ate porpoise flesh. But that queasiness didn't last long. The porpoise had become very special to me.

When we got back from vacation, I spent most of my time attempting to write a screenplay about the porpoise. I would tail him around the house, practically begging him for more biographical data so I could use it in my script. He wasn't impressed with my project.

"Who would pay to see a movie about me?" he would say.

When I told him to cut out the false modesty and reminded him of the success of other films featuring aquatic mammals, he would only sigh his now-famous (to me) sigh and say, "Well, maybe it would work. But Clifton Webb is dead and I can't imagine anyone else playing me."

After a few weeks at it, I realized my screenplay was getting nowhere and would continue to get nowhere with the porpoise's lack of cooperation. So I gave it up. I thought

[42]

he'd be pleased, but one day we were going to buy a humid-
ifier and he stopped in the middle of the avenue, turned to
me, and said:

"So you've given up the script already, eh?" He was
actually angry. "Why do you have to be such a quitter?"

At that moment he looked exactly—and I mean *exactly*,
despite his shiny black skin and blunt snout—like my father.
And after that moment our relationship changed. Oh, it was a
slow and subtle and often imperceptible change, but we both
knew, silently, that things had become different between us.

Things went along apparently swimmingly for awhile.
We did not speak of our differences. But I was growing restless with his constant presence, and I could tell (though he
took pains to hide it) that I was beginning to get on his nerves
for the first time.

He bought a painting, a seascape of the North Atlantic.
When I saw it I asked him if he didn't miss the ocean sometimes. He just sighed and looked at me as though I were a
child and said how he simply admired the painting as a work
of art. The porpoise pointed out the subtleties in the artist's
waves, but frankly I was oblivious to it all. I had other things
on my mind.

He was nailing the painting to the wall with his snout
when I heard a crash and a moan. I rushed into his room and
found that he had fallen off the stepladder. He claimed it was
nothing, that he just needed a few moments' rest, but his
color had changed. At dinner that night (he insisted on cooking it without my help) he was visibly worse. While he was
sitting at the table, I touched his forehead. He was burning
up. When I insisted he go into the bathtub and lie down, he
put up no resistance. I was surprised—and worried.

During the next few hours he was obviously getting
worse each moment. Still he said nothing: no complaints, no
moans—only that sigh of his. It was Saturday night, and I told

him that we would of course dispense with our usual joke-telling hour, but he insisted upon it. "Routine and discipline are good for you," he said. "Besides, I think you're just afraid of falling down laughing and cracking a rib tonight."

So we did it, had our joke-telling hour, though at my suggestion we did it in the bathroom so that he might stay in the tub and conserve his energy.

He surprised me by letting me go first. Unfortunately my mind was a blank.

Then, after a few minutes, I said without thinking, "Why should I become a butler to a fish?"

He shook his head. He didn't know. I could tell he was in great pain.

"Because," I said, "then I'd be serving a porpoise."

And he *laughed*. For the first time he actually laughed at one of my jokes. Owing to his condition, the laugh was a bit hollow, but was an unmistakable laugh nonetheless. Then he stopped and said:

"Icthylogically speaking, you know, that's incorrect."

I nodded. He looked so vulnerable in that bathtub. He tried to tell a few jokes, but he wasn't in his usual form and they weren't very funny. I laughed nonetheless because I had to. He didn't laugh at any other of my jokes, and finally the alarm went off, and our joke-telling hour was up. He told me to go watch a show he had earlier recommended, a show on public television. The porpoise said he wanted to rest; he had to get up early because he wanted to write a letter to the editor of the *Times*.

Five days later some men from the city came about the smell. Some of my neighbors had complained. Funny that it didn't bother me. I didn't go into the bathroom, telling myself that he needed a lot of rest after his fall. Just knowing he was nearby was enough.

As they were lifting him up and out the door, I overheard one of the men say they could use his fat for lubricating oil. I wanted to shout out something to that man. I wanted to hit him—but for some reason I just stood there.

18/X/1969

I turned 18 the summer of 1969. That summer I graduated high school. That summer it drizzled nearly every day,
if only for a few minutes. That summer they murdered
Sharon Tate. That summer Mary Jo Kopechne drowned.
That summer I saw my first X-rated movie.

I went alone. It was a particularly rainy day in early
August, when the Dog Days should have been. My friend
Yogi and I called drizzly summer days Spanish Fly Days
although we did not know why. Yogi was working at a day
camp being a counselor to retarded children who vomited a
lot and so I went to the Graham Cinema by myself.

The movie was called "Katherine of Oregon." The plot
was simple. A young girl with straight chestnut hair and a
beautiful body gets on a Greyhound Bus in Portland and
comes to the evil big city, the evil big city that I lived in. She
gets a crummy apartment with peeling ceilings and a mean
landlady. She gets fired as a waitress after another waitress,
an ugly one, trips her and makes her spill two trays of wine-
glasses. She gets involved with a boy of 18, a beautiful clean-
cut boy. It is the first love affair for either of them. They
are tentative, hesitant. He is more shy than she.

There is a scene in "Katherine of Oregon" where they
make love for the first time. They are in Katherine's fur-

[46]

nished room, on her creaking bed. The boy is lying face up on the sheets. He is muscular and his skin is clear. He looks shy. Katherine is coming into the bed and she lifts herself above him, then smiles a sort of beautiful smirk and goes down on him.

I wanted to freeze that frame in my memory: that frame of Katherine going down on the boy. At that instant I knew I would have to see the picture again.

I saw it three times that day and twice the next. Nothing that happened after that scene was particularly interesting to me. It was all sex with other men. Katherine discovers she is a nymphomaniac and gives up the boy for a succession of ugly older sock-wearing men who have pencil-thin mustaches. She gets kicked out of her apartment, becomes a prostitute, gets syphilis and dies in Bellevue's charity ward. Then a phony doctor comes on the screen and says that Katherine is just one out of many sad case histories in his files.

It was all bullshit to me except for that one scene. I loved Katherine of Oregon for that moment. I loved the boy too. They were both so sweet and innocent and high-school-erish; she with her cashmere sweater, her one good one, and the heart-shaped locket around her neck; he in his St. Francis High jacket, blue jeans and Keds.

The rest of the movie bored me. By the end of that week I had sat through it fourteen times and only enjoyed that one scene. I memorized her smile, his face, her tacky Bermuda travel poster on the wall behind them. I dreamed about that scene.

I watched the credits, too. I looked up the names of the actor and actress in the telephone book. She was the only one listed, and she was only listed by her initial. I would call her late at night when I could never sleep that summer and I would listen to her "Hello," so newly woken-up, so soft, and I would try to imagine her looking for me the way she looked for the first boy she loved in the movie.

Naturally I was a scared virgin.

I was supposed to start City University in the fall but
that was nothing to me. I became obsessed with that girl and
that boy and that scene. When the movie left the Graham
Cinema I followed it uptown to the Regency and to the
Valentine in the suburbs and I even took a Greyhound bus to
Delaware for a weekend to see it in some dilapidated theater
in Wilmington. Finally the movie stopped playing but I continued to think of it.

I had always been a good student in high school but
I couldn't concentrate on my classes at the University, not
even in English, which had always been my favorite subject.
We were assigned *The Great Gatsby* but I didn't read it. I
didn't understand one word of the class discussion on it until
the teacher came to the part where some character tells
another you can't repeat the past and the other character says
of course you can. "Now, is it possible for us to repeat the
past?" the teacher asked, trying to stir up interest in a flag-
ging discussion. All of the other students said that it wasn't,
so I raised my hand for the first time that semester and disagreed with them. "Why not?" I said. "It's got to be
possible, otherwise we're all doomed." The teacher looked
at me funny and asked another girl if Gatsby was doomed.
She hadn't understood anything I said.

I didn't really pay attention to anything that fall. It
still kept raining and the Haitian cleaning woman who worked
for my mother said it would never stop raining because when
the men walked on the moon that summer they upset the
balance of nature. My best friend Yogi took photographs of
the moon landing off the TV set with his grandfather's
Minolta. He gave me one, a split-screen picture of President
Nixon on one side talking on the phone to the astronauts on

the other side of the screen in their space capsule. The titles on the screen said WHITE HOUSE on one side and THE MOON on the other.

The actress who played Katherine of Oregon left the city in September. Her telephone was disconnected, her apartment sub-let to, of all people, my English professor. This really depressed me.

Yogi got worried about me. We hadn't really been close lately, not like we were when we were kids and fooled around and watched all the Yankee games on TV. I named him Yogi after his idol Yogi Berra and after a few years even his parents started calling him that. But we were drifting apart, all because of Katherine of Oregon. He couldn't understand what I saw in her. He finally went to see the movie with me and he didn't think much of it. "I've seen lots better," he told me. Yogi couldn't even pronounce *Oregon* right. He said "*Are*-gon" instead of "*Or*-egon." But he was still my friend and he wanted to snap me out of it. So one day we took acid together.

It was very wistful and blurry. Nobody jumped out the window. We just started drinking Boone's Farm Apple Wine, the whole bottle, and then we took off our clothes and stared up at the ceiling, us lying on the floor. We were giggling at nothing and Yogi came over and started wrestling with me. "Hey," I said, and I got surprised because I liked wrestling with him, I was getting a hard-on. Then he started looking like the boy in the movie and it was weird because he looked just like him except since he was stronger than me Yogi soon pinned me and he was on top of me looking down on me with that same beautiful arrogant smirk that Katherine of Oregon had in the movie when she went down on the boy. Yogi's body was hard when I touched it. He was on the fencing team. I almost said "I love you" to him but I didn't because

[49]

he would have thought that I meant him when I really meant
Katherine of Oregon or the boy or somebody, anybody else.
We giggled and wrestled and panted and finally lay back on
the floor sweaty and exhausted with laughter. The TV was
still on in the background somewhere. It was really late
because there was a picture of a menorah on it and some
voice-over was saying things like, "We pray for the quality of
wisdom . . . We pray for the intensity of devotion . . . We pray
for that kind of heroism that enables man to have mastery
over himself . . . " For a while I started thinking, wow, that's
the boy from the movie saying things but then another voice
came on and said that that morning's meditation had been
telecast with the cooperation of the New York Board of
Rabbis. After it ended there came a *bzzzz* and a test pattern.
I realized two things: that Yogi was asleep on the floor next
to me and that a hard rain was falling and had been falling all
the while. Because of the men landing on the moon, I
thought.

I wanted to put a blanket over Yogi and put my own
clothes on and stop that stupid *bzzzz*ing of the TV test
pattern, but I had no energy left. I tried to do it mentally,
like I sometimes did when I woke up in the middle of the
night having to piss: I would try to imagine myself getting
up and going to the bathroom and pissing. It always surprised
me that no matter how hard I tried to imagine pissing, it never
worked in reality. It was the same thing with Yogi and the
TV test pattern.

Eventually I fell asleep and dreamed not of Katherine of
Oregon but of Sharon Tate. Once I had masturbated to a
photograph of Sharon Tate in a bubblebath in a magazine I
found at the bottom of one of my father's drawers under
some business papers, some condoms, and 40,000 shares of
stock made out to a woman who was not my mother. In the
dream Sharon Tate came into my room with the bubbles still

clinging to her wet naked body and she started laughing at me. "What's so funny?" I asked her, kind of ashamed of what I had done. "You have an Oedipussy complex," Sharon Tate told me, and then she disappeared. After a few more dreams I woke up.

Yogi was looking at himself in the mirror and flexing. He was kind of embarrassed when he saw me looking at him but I didn't say anything.

"So," Yogi said. "What do you think of acid?"

I shrugged.

"It works better with time," he told me.

I told him I didn't want to do it again and he just put on his pants and walked out of the room disgusted with me.

* * *

That afternoon I called up Katherine of Oregon's old apartment, which now belonged to my English professor. I disguised my voice and asked her if she knew what happened to the previous tenant and how I could get in touch with her.

My English professor said that she had gone away with her boyfriend to the Coast and after some prodding she gave me their new number.

I called it long-distance. I got Katherine of Oregon on the phone and told her I loved her. She said she was living with her boyfriend. I asked if he was the same one as in the movie and she said no, he was a producer. I said I didn't care if she had a boyfriend. I told her I didn't want sex with her, that I was probably a homosexual anyway, that I really liked the guy in the movie better, but that I had to see her, I couldn't find *him*, I wanted to be with her, all I wanted was to be her best friend and if she said so I would take the next Greyhound bus to be with her. She accused me of being very sick and said she would call the police if I bothered her anymore. That's when I hung up.

I hadn't gone to school in weeks. It was November already and I was still wearing just a light sweatshirt. I had a
cold that wouldn't go away but wasn't bad enough to make
me have to stay in bed.

My parents began to be suspicious of me. One night I
came home very late in the rain and my mother didn't recog-
nize me when I rang the bell. She called my father to the
door and they were staring at me and asking each other who
the hell I was. I didn't know what was going on and I started
crying and saying stupid things like, "Can I get a motorcycle?
Can I get a helmet?" The boy in the movie had a motorcycle
and a helmet.

Finally they let me in, but on one condition: I would
have to get a job.

I called up Yogi and he said he was working at an under-
ground garage parking cars and that they were probably hir-
ing new help so I should go in in the morning. I did.

I walked down a sloping ramp and stood in front of the
window where the man was taking down names of all the
people who were on line waiting for jobs. There was a very
oddball-looking guy next to me, with a sort of short haircut
and a goofy expression.

The garage-owner at the window looked us both over
and said, "I'll only need you if you're lovers." The he chewed
on his cigar.

The other guy looked perplexed but I put my arm
around his shoulders pretty quickly and said, "*Sure* we're
lovers." He disentangled himself from me and ran away. I
was disappointed because it meant I wouldn't get the job and
then I heard a woman laughing at me.

It was Katherine of Oregon. She explained that her
career on the Coast wasn't going so hot and she had to go

back to working in porn films. I asked her what she was talking about and then the garage-owner guffawed and said, "What do you think we *do* here anyway, son?"

And they led me to this big room where they were making a movie. The set was Katherine of Oregon's creepy furnished room. Even the tacky Bermuda travel poster was on the wall. Yogi was in bed, his clothes off, waiting for her to join him.

She took off her blouse and handed it to me. I almost fainted.

Then I watched numbly as she got into bed with Yogi and he looked shy and beautiful and she went down on him with that same terribly wonderful sly smirk.

It's too late, I thought as I watched the scene happen all over again.

As if he knew what I was thinking, the garage-owner took the cigar from his mouth and said, "Don't worry, kid, it'll be your turn soon. Y'know, just living longer gives you confidence . . . That's one thing you'll find out here."

Sometimes I think he was right.

This happened in 1969, when I was 18.

WHAT GUILLAIN-BARRE SYNDROME MEANS TO ME

My son is sitting on my lap. His mother is sitting on the couch across from us. Her lover is next to her, his long legs stretching out on my floor. All four of us seem happy. They are a little tired from the long plane flight, but they have said that they do not want to go to bed just yet.

"So you're *sure* you're all better?" Anita asks me. She is playing with the long strands of her dark hair, shiny like an Indian's, and Detlev touches her lightly, meaning that she should stop it. She does, for a few minutes.

"I'm fine now." I wonder if they would be more comfortable if I turned up the air-conditioner. I am getting sweaty with Thomas on my lap. He doesn't seem real to me yet.

"All of this because of a flu shot," Detlev says. He shakes his head. Detlev has very long blond hair. It used to be straight, but now it is in some kind of a shag. He has recently shaved off his mustache, and I think he looks better without it.

I shrug. After all these months I am used to shrugging and looking comical when my illness is mentioned. I am enough of a *mensch* to see the humor inherent in the situation.

"I can't believe the government didn't take more precautions," Detlev says in his very good English. I am surprised that he is so fluent. "What do they call it again—Giscard d'Estaing syndrome?"

Laughter all around, even Thomas, who couldn't possibly understand. That *is* a new one. "Guillain-Barre syndrome," I say. "Viral encephalomyelitis to you biology people."

Anita shakes her head. I notice again how pretty she is. She has gotten less angular with the years. "It must have been so terrible for you, Peter." As always her concern is genuine. "To have it come on you so suddenly, the paralysis— all because of that stupid swine flu shot, it's so incredibly *stupid*. So American. Ford wanted to get reelected and he used this program to help him. In Germany a thing like this could never happen . . . "

On my lap my son is falling asleep.

Detlev agrees with Anita. "*Typisch amerikanisch*," he says.

I know I will hear those words a lot from them. I hope I will not hear them from my son.

I have put them all in my parents' old bedroom. Pretty cool of me. I have no trouble whatever falling asleep. The next day they all sleep late. Thomas seems to be getting a cold. "He was sneezing on the plane," Anita says. I go out to the drugstore to buy some children's aspirin, but Anita will not give it to him. I do not make an issue of it. He is such a lovely child. As I watch him sleep he becomes more real. He is four years old, my son is. While Detlev is shower- ing and Anita is having orange juice—"*wonderful* Tropicana, not the watery stuff we get in Hamburg"—I have the pleasure of watching Thomas wake up. His eyes are dark, like Anita's. He starts to cry, then stops. Thomas did not know where he was at first. "It's all right, Thomas," I tell him. "Go back to sleep."

"Okay, Peter," he says. When he talks English to me I could eat him up alive.

Hanging around the house.

Anita scans my desk. There is a paper stuck in the typewriter.

"Your dissertation?"

"No, an article Linda's having me do for *Seventeen*. Did I tell you they promoted her to editor of Mini-Mag? People keep moving on and Linda keeps getting promoted."

Anita is playing with her hair again. Detlev is on the couch, looking through my record collection.

"What's the article on?" she asks me.

"I'm kind of embarrassed about it. It's called 'Do Boys Like Independent Girls?' Remember, I'm writing for fifteen-year-old girls, not Mensa members."

Detlev looks up. "Do they?" he says.

"Who?" I don't know what he's talking about.

"The boys," Detlev says. He is holding an old Simon and Garfunkel album, *Bridge Over Troubled Waters*. "Do they like independent girls?"

"Oh, I suppose so," I tell him. I am aware that Anita is staring at me.

I laugh, look at Anita so she'll stop staring. "Well, I *liked* you," I tell her.

Detlev puts the record albums away. "Anita is surely independent," he tells me.

I look at Anita and start nodding. She seems almost shy.

In bed at night, I am angry. Angry at Anita mostly. Her being here has intensified what I felt when I was sick. It wasn't so bad for months before it. But when I was sick . . . I even wrote in a letter, " . . . when Anita left me . . . " But

[56]

she didn't *leave* me, we both left each other, it was mutual and mature and for the best. It had hardly bothered me that she took Thomas to Germany with her. Where else could he go? Anita and I weren't married. I didn't want to be a father, she wanted to be a mother, she wouldn't let me give her any money, she wanted to do it all on her own. *Till Detlev.* Was that what was bothering me? That she had someone, someone casually strong and domestic like Detlev while I had no one? When I became ill my mother had to fly up to New York to care for me. She missed the whole Florida winter and had to stay here for the big freeze.

"Why don't you move to Park Slope or Brooklyn Heights, places where you'd be more comfortable?" Anita had asked me. "Places with artists and young people. Why do you have to live in this strange middle-class Italian-Jewish neighborhood? It's a place for civil servants and families."

My parents left me the house, I told her. That was not an answer that satisfied her. She has left America and she cannot understand the security I derive from living in the same house I grew up in. When I jokingly said that she'd missed *Roots* on TV, she said, "Thank God, we heard enough about it as it was." I couldn't tell her I'd *liked* the show.

What I was angry about was not something personal. It was the fact that Anita had *escaped* the pressures the rest of us had to face after college: the recession, the nonexistent job market, the responsibilities of adulthood. After a few phone calls to friends, Anita said, "Everyone's turning into their parents." *Is that so bad?* Were our parents such bad people? Were those two sixtyish neurotic stylish people playing tennis in Tampa such terrible parents to me? Four years ago I would have said yes. But adolescent rebellion, even *post*-adolescent rebellion, has to end sometime. Unless you can escape and be a free-wheeling expatriate like Anita. What were the rest of us supposed to do, *run* away from it all?

My mother on the telephone.

"You're sure it's not too much for you?"

"No, Ma."

"They're not staying in Daddy's and my old room, are they?"

"No, Ma." A sigh, a lie. "I've got your room and they're in my room."

"How can they manage that?"

"Detlev sleeps on the floor."

A sigh from Tampa. "I don't know, it just doesn't seem right to me, him staying there. Doesn't it make you feel funny?"

"No, Ma."

"Is he German German? You said his father was a Nazi."

My fingers rap on the telephone dial. "He's very nice, really. A regular hippie, full of love for everyone, especially Jews. They're very guilty, big supporters of Israel. Anita says everyone there went wild over Entebbe."

"But the father? . . . "

"Ma, everyone that age was a Nazi. Look, Detlev's father was a prisoner of war in London. He hates the English, loves beer, sleep, soccer and television. He's a West German version of your brother Manny."

"Don't be so funny. I just don't like the idea of a Nazi in my house."

Her house. A signal to get off the phone. "Ma, we're on a long time . . . "

"Okay, Peter, but you take care of yourself and we'll be up to see you in June. Did I tell you Daddy's tests came back negative? He's walking on air."

"That's great." I notice Thomas has walked into the room. *He can walk.* I am still amazed at everything he does. I only wish he could speak English better. It's very easy to be bilingual at that age, I'd always thought.

[58]

"Peter, don't let them overtax you. You were just pretty darn sick, you know."

I know. I know. Would she like to talk to her grandson? But Thomas is not, to my mother's mind, a grandson of hers. Suddenly I don't like my mother very much and I say "All right, so long" quickly and hang up the phone.

I pick my son up in my arms. He laughs. He says something in German. I think he is trying to make me tickle him so he can laugh more. He has the cutest smile I've ever seen except for Anita's.

Don't let them overtax you. You were just pretty darn sick.

"Mehr, mehr," Thomas giggles, wanting more tickling.

I put my son down. "Later," I say. His giggles trail off.

Lunch at the seafood restaurant near the beach. Everyone is animated.

"Who is that woman you're doing your dissertation on again?" Anita asks me. I write her who it is in every third letter.

"V. Sackville-West." I say. The clams are good. Thomas seems to enjoy them, but I worry about his digestion. Does Anita?

"She was a lesbian," she tells Detlev. He nods. "Detlev likes Kurt Vonnegut." He nods again.

"So it goes," I say.

Detlev smiles. His smile is nice too. "Do you think I could see him while I am here?" he asks.

I shrug. "Search me."

Anita elbows Detlev. "I don't think Peter admires Vonnegut," she tells him.

"That's not true," I say. "I do like him. Anyway, I admire all writers. It's just as hard to write a bad book as it is to write a good one."

"Dissertations are hard to write too, eh?" Detlev says, and goes back to the clams. I don't think he meant it to be nasty, but I am defensive. I *have* been working on it for over two years.

Thomas babbles in German, with a little English thrown in. Detlev and I make him laugh and Anita tells us to stop it or he'll choke. So Detlev and I talk politics.

"Things are quiet in West Germany now," Detlev says. "Like here. Daniel Cohn-Bendit is a history professor now. Rudi Deutschke is in Italy, but of course his brain was injured when he was shot." Detlev himself is a socialist, dissatisfied with Chancellor Schmidt. Most of his friends are Marxists; some are crazy Maoists.

I talk about my own radical student days. A long time ago. "I never could chant," I tell him.

"It is so silly to be chanting," he agrees.

"Like, 'Hey, hey, LBJ, How many babies did you kill today?' "

"Or, 'Ho, Ho, Ho Chi Minh, NLF is gonna win,' " Anita says, wiping Thomas's lips.

"Ho Chi Minh was a pretty good guy," Detlev says.

"Yeah, he was." A short silence. "You know, in '41 he offered Ben-Gurion a Jewish home in exile in Hanoi."

"I never heard that," Detlev says. "Good for him." I wonder why I had to say that to him.

We walk on the boardwalk, but it is still a little too breezy.

"You're walking well," Anita says to me. We are holding hands. Detlev is in front of us with Thomas. They are talking about buying and flying a kite.

"I don't think I'll stay in Hamburg past next summer," Anita says. This surprises me. She knows this. "Oh, it's not that I don't care for Detlev. That's still the same. But how long can it go on? It's too comfortable, I don't — "

Her fingers are cold. "Just because you love someone doesn't mean you have to stay with them forever," I say. It sounds about right to me.

"Exactly," Anita says. I give her a mock punch on the arm and she kisses my forehead. "He reminds me of you," she says, motioning in front of us.

"Detlev?"

"No, *Thomas* . . . I think I've just about got it proven that stubbornness is hereditary and not environmental."

"Ah," I say. "He's a nice boy."

"I know we should talk more English at home, but it's hard. The other kids . . . "

I step on a plank that is rotting. Half the boardwalk seems to be rotting. "He should grow up independent, not like me."

"Girls like independent boys, huh?"

"I guess so," I tell her. And then we don't say anything. She stops us for a moment, tells me I have locked myself in a penitentiary of self-absorption. Then we walk on.

"I want to know about trends."

Detlev and I are sharing a joint. Anita, who has stopped smoking grass, is putting Thomas to bed upstairs.

"Trends," I say. "Mopeds."

"We have them already. For years. Anita cannot stand the noise."

"Laetrile," I say. "That's big now."

"What is that? Dope?"

"Sort of. Some people say it cures cancer and most of the doctors say it's a hoax."

"Big news, eh?"

I take a puff on the joint, pass it back to Detlev. "And I showed you those posters of Farrah Fawcett-Majors."

Detlev laughs. We turn on the TV and he cannot believe what is on the screen. We watch for an hour or so. Anita comes down and joins us. We have some beers—imported, of course. It's very familial.

"Why are all the shows taking place in the 1950's?" Detlev asks.

I laugh, start to choke on a swig of beer. "Those were the golden years," I say.

"For you?"

Anita breaks in. "Peter and I were too young to have much fun in the fifties."

Detlev leans over and kisses her on the mouth. Anita and I are on the floor. We are sort of touching one another.

"The fifties were a strange time in Germany," Detlev says.

Things are getting hazy and warm. Anita spills a little beer. Detlev teases her and we drag him from the couch onto the floor with us. The three of us find ourselves hugging each other. I keep telling myself I am amazed I am not uncomfortable. Anita is prettier than she ever was. She is wearing a sleeveless blouse and I notice that she no longer shaves under her arms. The hair is nice there. I realize what it is I like about Detlev: his *playfulness*. After a while we are all lying on the floor, all separate, all very still.

The dining room clock is ticking.

I hear Anita sigh.

There are things I would like to tell her and Detlev, but I do not.

After an hour I go up to see how Thomas is. Detlev and Anita are asleep on the floor.

When it happened—when I realized I couldn't move my legs—I thought it was a dream. The odd thing was I never panicked, not for a moment. It didn't seem like the kind of thing that could kill you, like cancer or heart disease or a stroke. It was just no feeling. So I couldn't move. I could reach for the telephone and call my friends and my doctor and my parents in Florida. Now it all seems like a movie in which I was the camera. It all happened around me.

Maybe it was because I was never really in danger. The paralysis never spread beyond the legs; my hands were always fine; my lungs were clear. Like most Guillain-Barre victims, I soon developed antibodies that cured the disease. It was only a virus, after all. The symptoms were unusual, a bit scary—though *I* was never scared. There are times when I think I wouldn't have minded so much if I had stayed paralyzed. It was only the anger that depressed me while I was sick, and the anger didn't really have anything to do with Guillain-Barre.

Two months before I had been in an air crash disaster rehearsal at Kennedy Airport. I was supposed to be a victim of the air crash, and I was placed on my back on the runway when the "disaster" began. Within three minutes I was on a stretcher and within another three minutes I was on an "operating table" in a mobile hospital. *Then* I was scared: everyone running about, the medics, the airport workers, the phony wounds, the "victims" and their real-sounding moans. It was all a charade, a rehearsal for a disaster, but I was more scared then than I ever was when the paralysis hit me.

These are things I think about in bed at night. My penitentiary of self-absorption.

I hate to say goodbye.

They want me to come with them, but I don't belong with them.

Yes, you do. No, I don't.

At the airport: "Why can't you find someone, then?"

Because all I'm looking for is a parent to cater to my

*needs, a child who can make me feel strong, a lover who will
always satisfy me, a magician to take away the pain, and a
goddess I can worship.*

Anita's lips: "Why do you always have to hide, Peter?"

Detlev's arm on my shoulder: "You would like it with
us."

Only my son seems unconcerned. Thomas likes me, but
at the moment he likes a Sesame Street book more. At least
it is English. Detlev gets down and imitates Ernie's gutteral
chortle. I say *"Coo-kie"* like the Cookie Monster. Anita just
tousles his hair.

In five minutes they are boarding the plane. How many
weeks has it been? How many days?

I walk into the El Avram Delicatessen, go over to the
counter. Donny, the Israeli who owns the deli, smiles at me.

"How are you, Mr. Sarrett?"

"How are you?" I ask him. Then I remember to say,
"Fine, just fine."

"So," Donny says. "You hear of the Israeli elections?
Good news, huh?"

"Donny, I think they've just elected a fascist."

"No," he shakes his head. "Begin's the only man who
could save the country. The rest of them are no good, weak.
They should ship them all here to America."

Like yourself, Donny, I think, but I do not say. He is in
New York to make money. All the Israelis say they will go
back after they've made their money. "Turkey, white meat,
on rye," I tell him.

He goes about slicing it with the machine, and I watch. I
try to avoid looking at myself in the mirror. I don't want to
see the double chin I am getting.

"What else?" he says.

"That's it."

"Your houseguests are gone?"

I nod. "Gone with the wind."

Donny wraps the sandwich. "Pickle?"

I nod again.

"Sour or half-sour?"

I still don't know which is which. But I have to say something, so I say *sour*. He slices the pickle into four sections, wraps it up, puts it in a bag with the sandwich.

On either side of the counter Donny and I move towards the cash register. "Two twenty," he tells me.

I give him two singles and a quarter, take the bag from him, wait for the nickel back.

"Hey," Donny says. "We don't take this here."

He returns what I had thought was a quarter. *1 Deutsch Mark*, it says, *Bundesrepublik Deutschland*. And a slightly different eagle.

"Sorry." I hand him two nickels and a dime instead, put the German coin back into my pocket. "It's worth more than a quarter anyway."

"Not here," Donny says. We stare at each other. "You all over your sickness now?" he asks me. "Everything okay?"

I try to be hearty. "Oh, I'm just fine. Terrific." He sighs and that is our goodbye.

At the door I hear Donny say, "Give Begin a chance, will you? Let's see what he's going to do first before you start calling him names."

"Okay, Donny." I smile back towards the counter. My hand is on the door. "Fair's fair."

HERE AT CUBIST COLLEGE

"There will be Kitty to contend with, and the Chancellor, of course," Olivia was saying. A dark, cool-eyed virgin, she taught Pronunciamento, a dialect spoken in the Dutch West Indies.

"I don't think you'll have much trouble with Bill," I told her. "Not while the school's in this legal hassle. He and old Armbruster are probably sitting around his office right now, comparing the length of their subpoenas." I waited a moment, two beats. "But, Liv, I can't support you on this. Not now. I'm sorry."

Outside my office, three Purerto Rican girls, in platform sandals and halters, were passing by, singing:

"We all live on a terminal moraine,
  A terminal moraine,
  A terminal moraine. . . . "

Olivia and I listed to them for a moment, then she looked straight through me.

"You don't think it will work?" she asked.

I sighed. "Rightness is all," I said, and got up to go to lunch.

My name has always been an interesting variable in my life. I don't wish to tell it yet, for I believe, as do many "primitive" cultures, that knowing a man's name gives you an inordinate power over his life. Call me Batman, if you must call me something, or Howard Johnson, or Matzoh-Tongue. Or call me Occupant, if you will; that's the name on all my junk mail.

Right now, sitting on my desk, there is a letter addressed to me, to Occupant, a plea for a contribution to the Council of Armed Rabbis. You may have it if you wish.

"You idiom!" she shrieked at me.

"You oxymoron! You anapest!"

Her screams could be heard in the halls, in the library, and out on N Street, Northwest.

"It's the revenge of biology," Olivia moaned.

"Take a Midol and keep quiet," I told her. She really was annoying me. She had her own office, but she refused to leave mine. She knew I disagreed with her about the reforms, but I couldn't get rid of her.

"Why didn't anyone respond?" she wanted to know. She had written up her 153-page proposal, and sent it out, with cover letters, to Gunnar Myrdal, Noam Chomsky, Jesse Jackson, Robert Coles, Buckminster Fuller, Linus Pauling, Mary McCarthy and Irving Kristol. No one acknowledged receipt of the document.

"It could be the vagaries of the mail system," I offered, much too generously.

Olivia held her abdomen. "I belong in a different century," she complained.

Now Olivia felt better. Our obscure gay playwright-in-residence—the Vagueleh, I call him—had joined her in her campaign to initiate the reforms. The Chancellor still took no notice, and the playwright accused me of poisoning Bill's mind against the proposal. He cornered me at a poetry reading.

"I look at you with loathing," he hissed at me, lisping. "And I tremble and curse." He actually did.

I responded: "There is no middle ground between us. I have led a bowdlerized life, while you have led a baudelairized one." That shut him up, and I was able to sit back and listen to the rest of the poetry.

First an elderly woman in Earth shoes read her stuff, which was pretty awful. One of her poems began:

"I am Christina Rossetti.
Ha! I fooled you! . . . "

Next came an effete young man with a Massachusetts malocclusion who read his epic about Holofernes' head.

Finally, a flannel-shirted, bearded, balding (quite quickly balding: strands of hair kept falling on his dickey) poet read some verses about the decline of the West as seen in the lack of satisfying rolls in the hay.

Some female graduate students in Comparative Myomancy were harassing this man: After he finished reading his work, they kept yelling out: "Author! Author!" and they tittered in their seats.

And Olivia wants more of this.

Did you take the letter from my desk? This one was also addressed to Occupant; it was an appeal to aid earthquake victims in Guatemala. Perhaps Olivia has taken it. She was infuriated when I told her I would send something.

"When it comes to earthquake victims, you're generous to a fault," she shrieked. "But where are you when it comes to victims of repression?!"

Yes, it must have been Olivia.

[68]

I went to the locker room before the big game. I figured it would take my mind off all this nonsense. The Coach, as usual, was very inspiring.

"Every time you think, you hurt the team," he told his players. "Every time you think you hurt the team, you're right," he added.

Finally, he whipped up their enthusiasm with a rousing cry of: "Gents, get out there and win this one for Edmund Wilson!"

And they did, too; that's good, old-fashioned know-how for you.

I am a virtual prisoner in my office again. This time it's another group of trouble-makers: the Neo-Christian Students Against Faculty Fascism have taken over the whole building. This God Squad, these latter-day would-be saints, are holding Kitty and the Chancellor hostage. And after all, what have they done? Bill may be a pompous Argentine, but he's no Eichmann. And poor Kitty; she's probably shivering in her sensible shoes, holding to her breast the two small children's books of which she is authoress (and *proud* to be called "authoress"): *Carl Otter Makes a Million* and *Mitchell the Llama's House*. I refuse to be bullied.

The police came and busted a few neo-Christian heads, so the siege ended. After all the excitement, I decided I could use some entertainment, so I went over to the college theater to sneer at the premiere of the Vagueleh's new play. Olivia was there, arm in arm with him; obviously she had ignored all small Krafft-Ebbing warnings.

Olivia and I smiled icily at one another as we met when we went over to greet our mutual cousin, Slim Celluloi, the film critic. He is her second, my first once removed.

"What are you doing here, Slim?" I asked. "Aren't you

usually at movie screenings? Or have you finally regained your senses?"

Slim smiled benignly. "I have been faithful to the cinema in my fashion. . . . But Olivia here persuaded me to see this young man's play. I hear it's going to be quite remarkable." Olivia fairly glowed with triumph.

"Don't forget, Slim, you're our *objective* co-relative," I cautioned him. "The curtain's not up and the jury's still out."

"Still the same old Batman," he said. What did he expect?

The play, if I can call it that, was of course abominable. Basically, it concerned an elderly city councilman named Schaffner who stands for all the old values; naturally, he's bitterly satirized (that Vagueleh is quite the Juvenal-delinquent). He meets up with this character named Hart, a bland young man who is an activist in the homosexual "rights" movement, and who tries to convince the councilman to vote in favor of some legislation his group is sponsoring. The councilman is not impressed with this guy's arguments, but suddenly the elevator in which Hart and Schaffner are riding crashes, and we are supposed to believe that they have now descended into Hell, where they are greeted by Karl Marx, who intends to help the incompetent Hart in gaining control of Schaffner's mind. This brain-washing set in Hell takes up the rest of the play, or at least all of the second and third acts, for I left, not waiting to see the fourth. I went home, defrosted some frozen jellyfish, and wondered how it has come to this.

Klingin showed up at my office. A porcine squidgereen, he edits *The New York Review of Gooks*, a racist newsletter with an anti-Oriental slant. For some reason he considers us brothers under the skin.

"Look, Johnson," he said. "We know it's an internanational conspiracy. They're all in it together."

"Get out of my office," I told him. "Go peddle your papers somewhere else, you anti-yellow journalist."

He gave me what he thought was a dirty look. "You've just made an enemy, Matzoh-Tongue," he said. Leaving my office, he murmured: "They say this guy's a Seraphic Jew."

Damn. Damn. Damn.

It's all over. The Chancellor has resigned. Kitty was taken to a sanitarium in St. Petersburg (I hear she thinks she's going to the court of Nicholas I). The rebels have destroyed my last two years' work, my notes for my monumental biography of impotent men throughout history. All that remains are an outline of a chapter on Carlyle, and a quote from John Randolph, his response to a fellow congressman who taunted him for his impotency: "Sir, you pride yourself upon an animal faculty, in which the negro is your equal, and the jackass infinitely your superior." It would have been an important book, and now what's left of it? These people are using the papers to make marijuana cigarettes; they're doing it with research papers, library books and even current magazines. I overheard one student telling another that his joint was out of *Time*.

Olivia comes in to gloat. Thankfully the Vagueleh is not with her.

"You've won," I told her. She surveyed the wreckage of my office.

"We can still use you, Jack," she said. (You might as well know it now—it matters no longer—my name is Jack.)

"Bushwa," I replied. "I'm getting out of here. You think I'm crazy, that I want to stick around while you people obnubilate everything?"

"Like what? The intellectual superiority of white Rhodesians?"

"Cut the crap, Liv. You know it was never like that."
"And now it never will be." With that, she left.

It's night now, and I'm just clearing up what remains of
this office and my life. Nothing means anything anymore:
aptitude, integrity, tenure. "Words, just words," Olivia said
to me—she who had once read a paper before the Modern
Language Association (it was on the Pronunciamento noun
"hwyl"; she was as eloquent as her subject then).

They've taken over; they occupy all the buildings, all the
open spaces. A plaza for everyone and everyone in his plaza.
Outside my window, boys—quite young boys, really—are
revving up the engines on their motorcycles, each one saying,
"I, too, can get an erection."

Well, once there was a volcano under my ice, but it is
burnt out. So why stay here any longer? But in a curious
way, I feel free.

WHAT ABOUT US GRILS?

1.

You can skip this first section if you like. I am merely beginning somewhere, "writing myself into a story." I don't know what this is going to be about yet. This is fiction without a net.

Here I am in print, skating the thin ice of ridicule. Confronted with another challenge of white space, I wonder if Yuri Gagarin felt like this in 1961, when he became the first man to orbit the earth. Our Hebrew school teacher told us not to be upset because Gagarin was a Russian: going into space, he said, was a great accomplishment for all mankind and would ultimately solve all our problems. Our Hebrew school teacher said that one of us would be teaching Hebrew school on the moon one day. As far as I know, nobody's done it yet.

Or maybe I should tell you something helpful, something that will help you live in this, Yuri Gagarin's, universe. (Do you remember that he died in a plane crash? Have you forgotten Yuri Gagarin already?) Here goes: in the summer, put a bunch of grapes in the freezer and serve them to kids; they're more nutritious than sugar ices, and they taste so good you'll want them for yourself. See? Does Joyce Carol Oates tell you things like that in her stories?

[73]

2.

A week ago last Tuesday, when I was denied unemployment insurance by the New York State Department of Labor and when I was told there would be no courses for me to teach this summer and when my mother told me I'd better do something to make money and when I threw a bottle of milk at her, screaming that I would rather die than work in a Burger King and what other job could I get, I held the contents of an entire bottle of Tuinals in my hand for three minutes.

An hour and a half after that I was in the Kings Plaza Shopping Center, three blocks from my house, ordering a cheeseburger with sauteed onions and an iced tea at Bun 'n' Burger. When the waitress gave me the sugar for the iced tea, I refused it, telling her, "That stuff's bad for you."

The indomitable human spirit.

3.

Last night at my girlfriend's house we were sitting on her bedroom floor taking apart the Sunday *New York Times*. Julie wants to work on a small-town paper some day. I tell her that newspapers are dying all over the country, that the *Times* has gone to cold type, laying off hundreds of linotypers, that in most cities there is a newspaper monopoly, that eventually people will subscribe to a newspaper service that comes over the cathode-ray tube of their home computer terminal, and besides, reporters don't make much money.

Julie countered or didn't counter by reading an "Author's Query" from the Book Review section. Somebody, it seems, wants to do an autobiography of William Ernest Henley.

"I bet you any amount of money it'll be called *His Unconquerable Soul*," I told Julie.

She just smiled. She would make a beautiful reporter for a small-town newspaper. Julie's image is now competent, but with panache. She projects it beautifully.

4.

In ninth grade we had to memorize "Invictus" and recite it before Mrs. Sanjour's English class. She told me I was too melodramatic. We also had to recite a soliloquy from "Julius Caesar" that year: I chose one of Brutus', when he was debating whether or not to join the conspiracy. I got a 98 on that recitation. They don't recite things anymore in school; that all went out with the 1960's, a decade I vaguely remember. Of course in 1965, when Julie and I were in Mrs. Sanjour's English class in Meyer Levin Junior High School 285 in Brooklyn, we didn't know we were in the 1960's, if you know what I mean. Julie and I keep saying we got the last good education in the public schools of New York.

Meyer Levin Junior High was not named after the novelist but the World War II hero, an airplane fighter pilot who had lived in the neighborhood. Meyer Levin's mother used to come to every graduation; she didn't look as though the school compensated her for the loss of her son. When I was little, I used to think the school was called "My Eleven." It was an excellent school, especially if you were in the SP program as Julie and I were. In Mrs. Sanjour's class we also read *The Odyssey* and had to write our own epic; we read Poe and Swinburne and Edward Arlington Robinson; we wrote short stories (Mrs. Sanjour ridiculed mine in front of the class: "Richard's 'The Bus Ride'—oh, that was a thrill a minute") and learned to read every section of the Sunday *Times*. We were quizzed on it Mondays.

Today Mrs. Sanjour teaches remedial reading. The school is mostly bilingual and 90% of the students are Haitians or Puerto Ricans. Mrs. Sanjour tells me her students are mostly comatose; and she likes them that way—it's better than violence. Mrs. Sanjour's teaching days are over, she says; now she baby-sits. She says she can't remember the short story that I wrote that she made fun of, but I do, vaguely: it had to do with a prejudiced woman talking against blacks on a bus. In the story I made it obvious that the woman was evil and banal.

That was a long time ago. I think—or would like to think —that my stories have been getting better. They're less obvious, though.

5.

For example, is this story about anything? Is it a story at all?

I don't know. I don't know.

Maybe after I finish writing it and then I read it, maybe then I'll know.

6.

I'd better work the title in sooner or later, so here goes.

Remember graffiti in the 1960's and the one that said MY MOTHER MADE ME A HOMOSEXUAL and the response under it, IF I GET HER THE WOOL, WILL SHE MAKE ME ONE, TOO?

When I was fifteen I wrote a play called, "If I Get Her the Wool, Will She Make Me One, Too?" You figure it out.

And Julie liked the graffito that said BROOKLYN BOYS LIKE GRILS. Naturally someone crossed out the word GRILS and substituted GIRLS. And just as natur- ally someone (me, I think) wrote underneath that BUT WHAT ABOUT US GRILS?

Have you figured it out yet? Three seconds I give you.

Good. I'm glad you got it.

7.

Another friend and former classmate at P.S. 203, Meyer Levin Junior High, Midwood High and Brooklyn College is Harriet. That's where Julie and I were last night, at Harriet's apartment in Greenwich Village.

Harriet is an editor at a women's magazine and was telling Julie and me about a story she had read. The story was submitted to her magazine and it was by Joyce Carol Oates and the manuscript looked like Joyce Carol Oates' agent had sent it everywhere. It was controversial because it was 59 pages long and kind of strong for Harriet's magazine. Harriet's managing editor knowing how much Harriet hates fiction (except mine, and that's only out of friendship) asked Harriet to make the final decision on the story. Surprisingly, Harriet loved it. But the managing editor decided not to use it anyway.

The moral of this story is that even good stories by Joyce Carol Oates get rejected for one reason or another.

The moral of this story is that final decisions are not always final.

The moral of this story is that Harriet talks a better story than I write.

One of these, anyway.

8.

So what *about* us grils?
(Counterpoint; repetition; irony)

9.

A 15-year-old boy is laughing so he gets shot in the head. The 13-year-old boy who killed him didn't like the sound of laughter. The Governor of New York State and the Republican candidate for his job call for life sentences for 13-year-old murderers. I myself, a gentle person, favor capital punishment.

What about us grils? Can't we laugh either?
(Gentle rhythmic thoughtfulness)

10.

This has nothing to do with anything, but then again, probably it does.

When my father was at his draft physical, one of them anyway, during World War II, he had to sleep overnight with hundreds of men in Grand Central Station. They had sleeping bags on the floor. At about one o'clock in the morning everyone heard an enormous fart from one side of the terminal. Then a loud voice announced:

"That came to you courtesy of Norman Greenstein!"

That is a true story, and mildly amusing. But my father makes it worse by fictionalizing the ending and telling us: "In the morning I offered him my conflatulations." Sometimes I do similar things with my stories.

11.

In suicide prevention circles, there is a cliche: "You can always kill yourself tomorrow." Even us grils can do that.

12.

"Pop, you're going to get better," said Julie's grandfather in 1936.

Julie's great-grandfather looked at him from the bed. He threw the covers off, revealing bare spindly legs. "With these matchsticks I'm going to get better?"

Julie's grandfather said nothing. Then Julie's great-grandfather spoke:

"I've loved life . . . but I've had to spend the last three months sleeping sitting up and the pain is unbelievable . . . "

"Pop . . . " said Julie's grandfather.

(To show I can write straightforward narration. Don't worry, I won't add my conflatulations.)

13.

Next to Julie's great-grandfather, in the Workmen's Circle section of Mount Lebanon Cemetery, is buried a woman whose tombstone reads BLANCHE "SPONGE-CAKE" BERNSTEIN.

Just one of us grils.

14.

With these matchsticks this story is going to get better? If you gave me some wool, could I write a better story?

15.

When Harriet confesses that she will not pick up black hitchhikers, do you have to admire her honesty?

When Mrs. Sanjour admits that she thinks about taking the gas now and then, do you have to feel sorry for her?

When Julie complains that graffiti depresses her, does she look as pretty or as competent as she did the moment before?

When my father tells a nice old story and ruins it with a bad pun, do I love him any the less? Any the more?

When Joyce Carol Oates writes a story, do you have to accept it? Or can you just think it's wonderful and say that's enough?

When I write myself into a corner, as I have done once more, do you have to give me credit for trying?

16,

Answers to the above:
No.
No.

No.

No. No.

No. I don't know.

Certainly not.

17.

When Yuri Gagarin was in junior high school graffiti didn't exist. Because he never saw it, that's why.

But neither did Yuri Gagarin exist in those days. At least not the Yuri Gagarin that I know.

18.

When Julie's great-grandfather was 18, back in Russia, he made a set of wings because he figured he was stronger than the birds. He jumped off the roof of a barn. He never got to flap his wings once. Luckily his sister had put straw where he fell. Julie's great-grandfather didn't hurt anything but his pride. The old folks called him a crazy boy after that.

People, including my father and Julie and Harriet, call me crazy at times. Sometimes it hurts and sometimes it doesn't. There are always Tuinals.

19.

I have to conclude the story here. I'm running out of ideas and Ko-Rec-Type.

"Ko-Rec-Type for Life," Harriet said last night to me and Julie. "Wouldn't *that* be wonderful?"

So I think this story has been about not committing suicide or something. I guess it's more complicated than that, but my mother just came in my room with my laundry to put away, so I can't bother thinking anymore. Or writing.

Just remember the frozen grapes. You'll really like them. Give them to your grils. They'll appreciate it. I know.

WHY VAN JOHNSON BELIEVES IN ESP

Van Johnson sat on his penthouse overlooking Central
Park and felt very whole. Does that make sense?

There was this very subdued but real feeling that he
could handle whatever was coming. Or if he couldn't handle
it, he wouldn't, and so what? He could see the Gulf + Western
Building. He could see into what was Charles Bludhorn's
window and he remembered good times spent there.

Van Johnson knew that Charles Bludhorn was his friend.
He loved Charles Bludhorn, even though Charles Bludhorn
was an ocean away.

Soon Van Johnson would be going to Elaine's; in the
morning, he would fly a plane back to California. He felt
secure with himself; he knew that he would take responsi-
bility for his needs and his life as best he could. New York
City was so beautiful at night, and he had memories of the
best times there. Van Johnson really felt sentimental about
New York City. His fingers ran through his red hair. He
supposed he had better stop his mental peregrinations. He
had to go to the bathroom.

At dinner, Van Johnson was quiet. Ethel Merman asked
him why.

"I've been with a different person every night for the

past two weeks," Van Johnson said. "So I'm tired."

"Oh," Ethel Merman said, looking at him with that look of hers.

"But I'm not promiscuous," he insisted.

Ethel Merman sipped her champagne. "No one's saying you were."

And then she yawned a great yawn.

When Van Johnson first left for Hollywood, his sister cried. He took her aside, away from the old grandmother who took care of them, and asked her, "Mabel, do you believe in dragons?"

That was an old thing between them.

"Yes," his sister answered. Then she didn't cry anymore and it was okay for Van Johnson to leave for Hollywood.

On a damp Friday night Steve McQueen drove his racing car past Van Johnson's house in Beverly Hills. Steve McQueen raced his motor and then shut it off. He found a phone booth and dialed Van Johnson's number. He knew it by heart even after all those years.

"Hi, it's me," said Steve McQueen.

"I'm with someone now," Van Johnson told him.

Steve McQueen nodded, but of course Van Johnson didn't hear him. He just hung up the phone.

Steve McQueen went back to his racing car.

In San Francisco a woman tried to assassinate Van Johnson. She shot at him while he was signing autographs in the lobby of the Mark Hopkins Hotel. But an ex-Marine named Sam Johnson saw what she was about to do and he gave the woman's arm a karate chop, thus deflecting her aim. She merely ruined a chandelier in the hotel lobby. They said she was a sick woman.

Sam Johnson, the ex-Marine, was a transsexual. He had been a woman named Sandy Johnson. All through her childhood she had always felt like a man. She knew she wasn't a lesbian. So when sex-change operations became more understood, she had one. Sam Johnson had an artificial penis.

Van Johnson, after his color returned, went over to shake Sam Johnson's hand. But then someone whispered in his ear that Sam Johnson was a transsexual and Van Johnson went pale again and just waved to him.

That night Sam Johnson was murdered. Some people think it was not just a coincidence.

Van Johnson joined Mensa because his little sister's IQ tested at 180 on the Cattell scale and he was jealous.

One time Van Johnson picked up a hitchhiker who claimed to be Patty Hearst. This was just after the real Patty Hearst was arrested in San Francisco. This was years before the woman tried to assassinate Van Johnson. The two women, though they didn't know each other, were distant cousins. Both of them were also distant cousins of Orson Welles. In *Citizen Kane* Orson Welles played a character who was based on Patty Hearst's grandfather, so in a way it made sense.

Here's how the conversation went between Van Johnson and the girl who claimed to be Patty Hearst:

VAN JOHNSON: You're not Patty Hearst. What do you think, that I just fell off the turnip truck?

HITCHHIKER: Excuse me?

VAN JOHNSON: I said, "What do you think, that I just fell off the turnip truck?"

HITCHHIKER: Really, man, I am. They got the wrong chick in San Francisco. Listen: SLA all the way!

[83]

VAN JOHNSON: That doesn't prove anything. Anybody can say, "SLA all the way!"

HITCHHIKER: Anyone can say they just fell off the turnip truck.

VAN JOHNSON: That's true.

She got out of the car at Santa Monica Boulevard. She smoked Winstons and was ten pounds overweight.

Once Van Johnson had a dream about her. He told it to Orson Welles.

Van Johnson began to write poetry. He worked in conventional forms at first, in an anonymous formal poetic manner. Liberace said that Van Johnson's early work was "skillful, well-placed . . . but not distinctive." Lucille Ball said the same thing.

As Van Johnson's career as a poet advanced, he became fascinated by the use of the spoken voice in poetry. He liked to write dramatic monologues. His favorite poem of Robert Browning's was "My Last Duchess." Van Johnson wrote a poem about a crippled World War II Air Force veteran who regained the use of his legs following an operation by a surgeon who looked like Ruby Keeler. The first line of the poem was: "Those are my last crutches hanging on the wall . . . . "

This poem was anthologized in *The Best-Loved Poems of the American People*. Van Johnson's sister had a dog-eared copy by her night-table. On top of it was her teddy bear.

When Van Johnson saw his grandmother for the last time, she was senile and in a nursing home.

"So, are you working now?" the old lady asked him.

"I'm an actor," Van Johnson told her.

"What'd you have for lunch?" the old lady asked him.

"Um . . . roast beef," Van Johnson said.

"What does your sister do?" his grandmother asked.

He didn't have the heart to tell her. His sister had become a poet, too. Their grandmother had always hated poets. "Scum of the earth," she used to say about them.

At the bar Evelyn Keyes pretended not to know Van Johnson. This was because he had seen her in a doorway in Greenwich Village. Evelyn Keyes had been drunk that day. So when she ran into Van Johnson at the bar, she was ashamed.

Van Johnson acted like a gentleman. He pretended he didn't know Evelyn Keyes from Adam. So did Ethel Merman.

"What do you do for a living?" asked the reporter from the *National Enquirer*.

"Mostly I act," Van Johnson told him. They were in his New York penthouse.

The reporter asked questions for a living. This was his next one:

"Do you believe women should get equal pay for equal work?"

Van Johnson nodded affirmatively.

"Do you ever think to yourself, 'What am I doing here?' "

Van Johnson said yes.

"Do you believe in ESP?"

"I do," Van Johnson said.

"Why?" the reporter asked.

"Because I like the sound of it." That's what Van Johnson said. The reporter smiled. It was the best answer he'd had all year.

LINCOLN'S DOCTOR'S DOG

First of all, congratulations on your good taste in reading this story. So few people today have the patience or the ability to appreciate good contemporary fiction. Most people are lazy and just plunk themselves in front of the TV set night after night, watching the same old trash. This story is going to be infinitely superior to anything you could watch on TV.

But as this story may take up a considerable stretch of your time and mental energy, and as I know how things get backed up in our hectic everyday lives, I'd like you to consider if there's something more important that you should be doing at the moment. Is there an old friend whom you ran into a while back whom you promised to give a call "one of these days" and never got around to it? Give them a call now, before you read this story. You can never tell: the other person might be able to help you one day. It is wise not to let friendships deteriorate.

Are you reading this story to escape from your problems? Don't. That does neither of us any good. Readers of this story must give it their undivided attention, and it is unfair to me as the author to bring along all your unsolved personal problems to the reading of this story. I just want to make sure that no one is reading this for the wrong reasons. What's the thing that bothers you every night just before you go to bed? Go try and work out whatever is bothering you. Talk it over with your clergyman, perhaps, or a sensitive and non-judgmental neighbor. Then you can come back to my story with a clear mind. I guarantee that you'll enjoy it much more that way. In fact, anyone reading this story who does not get any enjoyment out of it may be well advised to seek professional guidance. Lack of appreciation for a story of such obvious high literary quality may be a warning signal that one suffers from serious and deep-rooted emotional difficulties. Perhaps there are important problems which you have been repressing. Everyone should love this story. Hence, its eponymous hero, Lincoln's doctor's dog. Remember that old saw about books and stories that sell well? They said that the biggest sellers were about Abraham Lincoln, the medical profession, and dogs. Well, I have rolled them all together in this little fictional piece about Sparky, Lincoln's doctor's dog.

How are you enjoying the story so far? If you don't like it, maybe it's because you'd really rather be having sex right now. Why aren't you out (or in) having sex? Check your appearance in a full-length mirror. Are you attractive enough to appeal to one of the opposite sex? If you don't feel like having sex at the moment, ask yourself why. Lack of sexual desire often indicates a serious physical problem. However, don't worry unduly: we all get that "I just don't feel like it" feeling every once in a while. Even Lincoln's doctor's dog felt like that sometimes—and he fathered twenty-three puppies.

(Some people may wonder why I am writing this instead of having sex right now. Let me assure you it is not because I am unattractive. Quite the contrary is the case. But you see—and I hope I don't lose any readers over this simple declaration of honesty—my tastes run to 14- and 15-year-old boys, and they are hard to come by, and when I do have sex with them, I feel this crushing guilt afterwards and I can't handle that. Lincoln's doctor's dog knew all about guilt, and I'm sure he would have advised me to do just what I'm doing; namely, sublimate my deviant sexual urges by writing a decent story about a dog rather than sodomizing young teenagers. Besides, I am a frail man and I often get beaten up by these youngsters.)

I'm sure that as much as Lincoln's doctor's dog would have loved for every one of you to read this story about him, he'd like to see me make one last attempt to weed out those readers who really should be doing one of the very few things more important than finishing this story. That is, interacting with another human being—and I'm not talking about sex here, either. Have you noticed how the art of conversation has died out since the days of Lincoln's doctor's dog? Are you reading this story all by yourself? Why not read it aloud to a friend or relative? Are you neglecting your wife or husband or children to read this story, selfishly excluding them from the pleasure derived from it? Have you called your mother lately? If you are of the Jewish faith, do so immediately. Christians may wait until after finishing this story to call their mothers. (Lincoln's doctor's dog was a Christian.) If your mother is dead, think about her for a moment before continuing on with your reading. It is true, you know: no one ever loves us the way our mother did. Let me tell you, my mother was a saint.

Lincoln's doctor's dog's mother was a bitch. Her name was Fido, and she was a German shepherd belonging to Mrs. Idelle Morris of Hagerstown, Maryland. When Fido gave birth to a litter of fine puppies, Mrs. Morris gave one to her trusted family physician, Dr. Rumney, who later became the physician to President Abraham Lincoln. Dr. Rumney named his dog Sparky. Sparky was a lively pup, and grew into a sensitive yet strong dog, always capable of playing upon the weaknesses of others. President Lincoln, who suffered with bouts of severe depression, was treated by Dr. Rumney; Sparky often accompanied his master to the White House on these occasions. In no time he became a favorite of the Administration. Sparky was a constant tonic to the Chief Executive. Active, excitable, ubiquitous, he sometimes sat in on Cabinet meetings and war strategy sessions. When the President was assassinated, it was Dr. Rumney who failed to save his patient, and it was Sparky, along with Secretary of War Stanton, who made the arrangements for the state funeral. There exists a Matthew Brady daguerreotype showing Sparky conferring with General Grant. When other Army officers complained that Grant would not tell them about troop movements in the final days of the Civil War, General McClellan told them: "Neither will he tell me. That damned canine is the only one to hold Grant's confidence."

Eventually, Sparky married and was elected Governor of a small Midwestern state. He became a national figure for his leadership in the Anti-Seance Association. Sparky was known for his religiously fatalistic approach to life; this was particularly unusual at this time, especially when one considered Sparky's humble origins. President Hayes appointed Sparky Minister to Nicaragua, and Sparky's heroic efforts in the great Managua earthquake are legendary to this day. His wife Abigail, who was of weak constitution, died while on a goodwill tour of the Mosquito Coast of Central America. After a decent period of mourning, Sparky remarried, this time the eldest daughter of an unsuccessful merchant seaman. His new wife soon became quite ill with an attack of pleurisy. Sparky went down to the local drugstore and asked the pharmacist what medicine was most efficacious in curing that malady. At this point in time Sparky was a character in my famous 1967 novel, *Jerome Klinkowitz, R.Ph.* Those of you who wish to follow this part of the story will have to read the novel, available from its publisher, the Houghton Mifflin Company, for $7.95. *Jerome Klinkowitz, R.Ph.* is the story of a registered pharmacist. The story begins in 1941 when Jerome is in the Army as a pharmacist technician and ends in 1966, after many years of interesting experiences dealing primarily with his practice of pharmacy. The novel tells of the rigors of going through pharmacy school and of taking the Maryland State Board Examinations. With all due modesty, I must say that this story does for the pharmacist what *The New Centurions* did for the policeman. It presents the pharmacist as a person doing a necessary, useful job and tells of the problems faced by every pharmacist. Not only does the reader enjoy an interesting story of Jerome Klinkowitz, he also gets a very good insight into the laws regulating the practice of pharmacy and how it affects each reader's life directly when he or she should require prescription medication. *Jerome Klinkowitz, R.Ph.* is a fictional story based on fact, as is this story about Lincoln's doctor's dog. Most of the events portrayed both in the novel and in this story you are reading now are basically factual, with license taken to change or color the incidents so as to present a more interesting story.

After spending what seemed 138 unendurable pages trapped in the novel, Sparky managed to escape back into his own story in what proved to be an inopportune moment. For when he returned home, he discovered that his second wife had merely been feigning pleurisy as a ruse so she could run off with her own half-brother, an itinerant piano tuner from Jacksonville. And Sparky's great wealth had been taken. He did not have a cent in the world, or anywhere else. The new Democratic Administration in Washington was not familiar with Sparky, so there was no patronage. Dr. Rumney was long dead. So Sparky went to bed for five of the next six years. It was during this time that Sparky had his famous clairvoyant dream. Sparky's dream foretold the invention of the automobile, the rise of the atomic age, and Clement Attlee's surprising victory over Winston Churchill in the 1945 British elections. Sparky awoke a new dog. He traveled far and wide, giving people advice on how to live the good life. Some of Sparky's tenets are still with us today: "Use no artificial devices to awaken one's self. . . . Do not attempt to fool infants with false smiles. . . . Believe in something strongly; anything will do. . . . OXO, OVO, and OZO are good names for products because they resemble the human face. . . . Engage in purposeless activities daily." At the ripe old age of death, Sparky's mission in this world was at an end. Thus ended the travails, triumphs, and tragedies of Lincoln's doctor's dog.

   Some of you, I know, must be agape with awe right now, wondering how an author comes up with ideas for such excellent stories. The answer is simple: determination, hard work, discipline, creativity, a sense of confidence in one's self, a good head on one's shoulders, the ability to guess what the large majority of readers will find fascinating. Often I am asked what an author's day is like. Since the story of Lincoln's doctor's dog ended a bit earlier than I had originally planned, I have some time left over to tell you now what my day is like.

   I wake up generally around ten or eleven, following Sparky's dictum that alarm clocks are harmful to one's health. I do my calisthenics, shower and shave, eat a hearty but low-cholesterol breakfast, and am usually out of the house by early afternoon. All this while my mind has been racing, thinking up stories to amuse and delight the general public. Then I usually hang out around the school play-ground and watch the boys play basketball; on warm days, they take off their shirts. Then I go to a diner for lunch; I sit at the counter by choice. I really do prefer the counter.

Often I have shopping to do next. My mother, God love her, trained me to be an excellent consumer. Then I go home and get down to my serious business: writing. I write for several hours straight, picking up steam here and there, losing ground at a few points. If I am writing a love story, I often interrupt my writing to watch a soap opera or two. Some of their plots aren't half-bad, but they need the touch of a master stylist. I usually don't have much trouble with interruptions; my friends have enough sense not to call or visit while I am engaged in my work. And then, after awhile, a story is produced. There is no joy on earth like finishing a story, imagining how it will look in print, and thinking of the check that will come—a symbol of the regard in which creative people are held in this society. (If only Sparky were alive to see this day.) After writing a story, I have a TV dinner usually (I never learned my mother's cooking secrets) and write letters or make telephone calls. After finishing this story, I got out the Manhattan telephone directory and dialed the number of Theodore Solotaroff, the editor of the *American Review*. Here's how the conversation went:

Me: May I speak to Mr. Solotaroff?

Mrs. Solotaroff: This is *Mrs.* Solotaroff.

Me: *Mr.* Solotaroff, please.

Mrs. Solotaroff: He's not home now.

Me: Well, you can tell him that I've just written a masterpiece and he will print it and. . . .

Mrs. Solotaroff: Please submit it to his office, not to his home. His office is 666 Fifth. . . .

Me: Yes, I know. This phone call will make you famous too.

Mrs. Solotaroff (laughing): Okay. Good night.

Then I hung up and finished writing the story by including my phone conversation at the end of it.

Now I'm going to bed. I'll sleep well, knowing I've done

[92]

another good day's writing and that people everywhere will undoubtedly enjoy my story of Lincoln's doctor's dog.

THE SECOND PERSON

Doctor Golden is examining you.

She is old enough to be your mother.

She wears tinted eyeglasses. Her skin is leathery. She has spent too many summers sunbathing. Around her neck the skin is like crepe.

The third finger of Doctor Golden's left hand has no first joint. Where the finger has been amputated the flesh mushrooms out slightly. This little overhanging ball of flesh is a different texture from the rest of the finger. Doctor Golden's hands are cold.

During her lifetime Dr. Golden has faked orgasms, failed to keep appointments, been unable to stop perspiring.

Doctor Golden reminds you of your dead mother, but her manner is more controlled, tighter. She speaks in staccato sentences, as if she were uncomfortable. But you know she is not. It is you who are uncomfortable.

You believe you detect a slight odor of marijuana in the examining room. You breathe in, you breathe out—as Doctor Golden requests you to. You cough, you look into her eyes. You let her take your blood pressure: pumping and release.

"What is it, do you think?" you ask, a tentative question.

Doctor Golden says "Shhh," listens to your heart beat,

smiles and says, "You may get dressed now."

You are alone now, and naked.

Her white lab coat on, she sits behind her desk. It is a steel desk, very modern and businesslike. There is a paper-weight made of bluish glass in the form of a seal on Doctor Golden's desk. In another corner of her office there is an old rolltop desk which contains nothing. The rolltop desk is just for show.

Doctor Golden taps her pencil, says nothing. She is waiting for you to speak first.

"Well. . . . " You acquiesce. There is a slight lilt to your voice, as if you were going to tell a joke or a story.

She smiles that incongruous smile again. Her office smells of soap. A few of her greying curls are out of place. She shakes her head, slowly, from side to side, as though examining her office for flaws.

Finally: "I don't think it's somatic."

You flinch, then you smile. Not Doctor Golden's kind of a smile, but a nervous, blustery smile. You stutter when you say: "You didn't find *any*thing?"

"Nothing that would justify your symptoms," she breaks in. This Doctor Golden is a quick woman. One to be mistrustful of. You wonder how many men she has loved, how many women. On her amputated finger there is a narrow gold wedding band. So she must be a widow, at least.

You whine. "But I'm so *tired* all the time. . . and the headaches. . . . " A mistake, of course. Because now Doctor Golden can say:

"It's just the depression, after all." And she wipes you away with a blink of her eyes. She looks at her desk calendar. After a moment she taps her pencil again.

You close your own eyes. You press in with the thumb and forefinger of your right hand. Doctor Golden is gone,

replaced by an orange-red mass before you. In a faraway
voice Doctor Golden is speaking. Something about pressure
and stress and coping techniques. A prescription of some
kind, obviously inadequate. A remark, a warning about mis-
use of tranquilizers. You let go of your eyes and the orange-
red blob dissipates. You can see Doctor Golden in front of
you, coming into focus. There is a prescription in her left
hand. She is standing up. Her right hand is partially out-
stretched. Doctor Golden means to end the visit.

You shake her hand mechanically. "Couldn't it be the
blood sugar?" you say, but before you can finish, she is
already smiling viciously, shaking her head no.

Before long you are outside her office, paying the
yellowish, pockmarked secretary for the visit. Twenty dollars
this time, because it is not an initial visit. Initial visits with
Doctor Golden cost more.

You are working. Grudgingly, listlessly—but there is
little else you can do. Doctor Golden has said it: you are not
sick. And so you must work. At the switchboard life moves
fast. Calls come in from everywhere. You must move fast
and talk swiftly.

A call from Rhode Island, a muffled man's voice. "My
girl and I have to get married. We need a justice of the peace.
Does that classify as an emergency?" You decide that it does,
you put the call through. These days only emergency calls
may go through.

"My male parent has died. I need an ambulance."
Another emergency. Everyone sounds so composed. You
are in control, yet you are the one who worries most about
going on. But you must go on, for there is nothing wrong
with you. Doctor Golden has confirmed this. The problem
is not physical. It must be mere inertia.

Another call, a woman with a Slavic accent. "Why am I
here?" she wails. She wails so loudly it hurts your ear.

[96]

You look up the answer in the book and tell it to her: "Because a particular sperm fertilized a particular egg."

Satisfied, the Slavic woman hangs up.

The phone does not stop ringing. "I want to have a long discussion about who will go to heaven and who will go to hell," someone asks.

"I'm sorry," you say, trying not to sound sympathetic. You do your job to the best of your ability. "I can't help you now, sir. Call again when this emergency is over, will you, and I'll see if I can get you a line."

"How long will that be? Till this is over?"

You sigh at the stupidity of this man. "There's no telling, sir." And you hang up quickly, pretending that this call never happened.

You let the phone ring for a while as you swallow your pills. Three a day—so you take all three at once. Some people are so foolish, like that last man. They don't realize that life is a constant emergency.

Another phone call. A youngster, it sounds like. "I'm scared . . . " A very small voice.

"What are you scared of?" you ask the child.

Silence.

"What are you scared of?" you repeat.

The child says nothing.

You cluck your tongue. "According to regulations, I can only ask you one more time. Now what are you scared of?"

A pause, a gathering of breath. "That I'm crazy," the child says.

You start to laugh and immediately hang up.

On your break you look in the mirror. Stick the tongue out to look at it—it's coated white. There is a sprinkling of blisters at the corner of your lips. How could Doctor Golden say she found nothing? Then you remember you forgot to tell her about your limbs always falling asleep. So often you get that pins and needles sensation, the numbness. Poor circulation—surely that is something for Doctor Golden to consider. If you did not enjoy the numbness so much you would call her right up again.

You know, deep down, why you cannot be sick, why Doctor Golden will not tell you so. It is because you are necessary. You perform a vital function in this climate of emergency. As your neighbors keep telling you, "I'd be damned *proud* to say I do what you do." Yet none of them ever volunteer.

Back at the switchboard, calls are coming in furiously.

"Most good things have passed me by," someone complains, and you take down their name and number. You promise you will have the proper people call her.

Another person phones and says, "What I need is someone to teach me how to breathe properly. Otherwise I will die."

You tell them you will try to help them after the emergencies are taken care of. Perhaps in a few months.

An old woman calls, says that she wants to commit suicide.

"I'm sorry," you say. There is nothing else to do but hang up.

Your head is pounding. There must be a tumor. Doctor Golden must have overlooked something. How can you function like this?

Another call: "I want to save the world, but I don't know where to start."

You sigh. You look into the book. There is no specified response to this. You are so tired you do what you are not supposed to do and you say:

"I don't know the answer to that. I'm sorry." And you

begin to weep.

Someone is lifting your eyelid. The world is coming in. An amputated finger with a narrow golden wedding band. Doctor Golden. Her hand. Your head. Lying down. She is looking at you with an unfamiliar look. Doctor Golden looks puzzled.

"See, I *told* you. . . . " you begin to say, but she hushes you.

Her hands smell of soap. Behind her tinted glasses she has bluish eyes. Your eyes are open. But it hurts to keep them open.

There is satisfaction somewhere inside of you. Doctor Golden was incorrect. Now even she must apologize. You are gravely ill. It is so good to know. Now you must get proper treatment.

"Can you sit up now?" she asks you.

"I think so." Slowly you do. It is the examining room again. The smell of marijuana is gone. A floral air spray has replaced it.

Then it comes: that same irritating smile of Doctor Golden's. One cannot imagine anyone else smiling in that manner. And her mouth opens, you can see the fillings in her teeth, and you hear her say:

"It's nothing. You took too many pills."

Stunned. Still she can say that? You hold up three fingers. "Only three. . . . "

Back and forth shakes Doctor Golden's head. You remember: tomorrow is the anniversary of your mother's death.

"There's nothing wrong with you," Doctor Golden says. "You may go back to work in a small while." Everything is so precise.

Close your eyes. Listen for other sounds. Do not hear

Doctor Golden's voice. Forget about the switchboard. See if you can feel your tumor or your heart condition or your fever. Do not accept what is around you.

But it comes through nevertheless. And you know that there is little you can do to change what is. Doctor Golden has done her job. Now it is up to you to do yours.

HOW NOT TO WRITE A NOVEL

It was the summer my mother finally read *One Hundred Years of Solitude*. I had been trying to get her to read it for years, but the cover of the Avon paperback turned her off. "Too much like Rousseau," she told me. "*Henri* Rousseau," she added, as if I didn't know. While she and my father were in Curacao, I ordered the hardcover from the Book-of-the Month Club, and when she got home, it was waiting for her on her dresser. I had taken the dust jacket off and given it to my friend Jerry to hang up in his bedroom. Jerry *liked* Henri Rousseau.

My mother clunked the novel shut in late August, the weekend before Labor Day Weekend. She clunked it shut loudly, for effect, as some of us sat by the pool. My father was reading the Real Estate section of the Sunday *Times* and he looked up when he heard my mother shut the book.

"No good?" he asked. His half-glasses made him look wise and settled, things he was not.

My mother rubbed her nose with her palm; then she realized she had suntan oil on her palm and rubbed it off on a beach towel. "I think Richard should write a book like this," she announced.

I laughed.

My father half-sighed and went back to his Real Estate

[101]

section. His own father had died at the beginning of the summer and this had made him aware of his own mortality.

My brother and his girlfriend began playing backgammon. My father put on some *salsa* music from the Spanish radio station—where he learned to like that stuff, I'll never know. My mother gave herself back up to the sun, lying face-up, corpse-like, on the redwood chaise lounge. She began to hum. I couldn't make out what she was humming above the *salsa* music. She was still holding the novel on her stomach.

I went inside to the bathroom, put my wet trunks and jockstrap into soapy water in the sink, sprayed deodorant under my arms, put on a pair of cutoffs and a tank top. When I went outside again, I was drinking iced tea. Both of my parents were asleep.

Later, that night, after we had all sat around the kitchen eating Chinese food and watching *60 Minutes*, my mother turned to me and said, "So? Do you think you'll do it?"

I knew what she was talking about. "I have nothing to say," I told her.

"Sure you do," she shot back.

My father had a coughing fit—he smokes too much, of course. "Just write about things you know and you'll find your theme," he said, and then he resumed his coughing fit.

"Just write about us, your family," my mother told me. "It'll all get changed around anyway, like in Marquez's book."

"*Garcia* Marquez," I corrected her.

"Well, just *do* it," she said.

My father brought out a game called Triple Yahtzee, a game my parents enjoyed, and they began playing it. It was played with dice. I never understood Triple Yahtzee so I went upstairs, masturbated, and fell asleep.

I dreamed I was in Rousseau's painting *The Sleeping Gypsy*, or perhaps it was Hicks' *The Peaceable Kingdom*. The only other person there was the novelist John Gardner, who was riding a motorcycle. He came over to me and I could see his long blond hair shining in the moonlight. He was smoking a pipe. He carried sheafs of paper, things I'd written.

"You'll never make any money writing this stuff," John Gardner told me. He let go of the papers gently and they wafted all over the silent jungle. "You'd better write a *real* novel." Then he went away. He left his motorcycle behind.

In the morning I got a letter from an editorial assistant at Harper and Row. She had read one of my stories.

"This is just a small note to let you know that if you have a novel completed, in progress, or even just still in mind, Harper and Row would be delighted to consider it for publication," she wrote. "Your writing suggests to me that it would be well worth your *angst* indeed to tackle the larger scale and other dimensions and demands of the novel form, if you haven't already. If you have, may we see the result?"

That afternoon, a Monday, I sat down at my typewriter and began writing my novel.

Since a novel must begin somewhere, and since my mother has suggested Garcia Marquez as a model, I begin my novel a century ago. The first sentence of my novel is:

It starts in 1881, a year that can be read backwards as well as forwards.

The first event in the novel is the assassination of Czar Alexander II by revolutionary terrorists. The modest liberalism of his regime comes to a halt and within a month a wave of pogroms spread across the Pale of Settlement. Eight men live in the Pale with their families; all are Jews; all are my great-great-grandfathers. Their names are Katz and Katzman and Ginsberg and Gelfand and Saretsky and Shapiro and Cohen and Slutsky, but their names do not matter. It is their sons, my great-grandfathers, who decide to leave Russia. This is later on, at the turn of the century. I chronicle their journeys briefly; it has all been done before.

I decide to use people's real names in my novel. There seems no reason to change them. I don't want to have to use a chart with everyone's real name on one side and their character's name on the other. This will slow me down. And as I am already in my late twenties, I can't afford to waste time.

It is Monday night and I am already sixty pages into the novel. It is going to be a big novel, one with big themes and lots of characters and many interesting events. I skip dinner and keep on typing.

I tell about one of my great-grandmothers being killed by Cossacks, and her husband going to America and remarrying, and sending for his children and his parents later. I tell about another great-grandfather, an orphan, working his way up to become one of the richest landowners in Poland. I tell about another ancestor who was a Marxist and a bomb-thrower and an intellectual and a maker of violins. He marries my great-grandmother when she is fourteen years old; he sees her swinging on a gate. I briefly sketch these years; it has all been done so much better already.

Next I take my grandparents, have them meet each other, have them marry. (It is Tuesday morning already, and I am still going.) My father's mother and my mother's father live next door to each other in the tenements of Brownsville. They marry my father's father and my mother's mother because these are the people whom they love. Each of these couples has two children, an older daughter and a younger son. Symmetry makes for an interesting novel; these things also happen to be true.

Both sets of grandparents go through the Depression. My father's family, the Ginsbergs, are quite well off. They always have a car and they always have a house. The Sarretts, my mother's family, are not so well off, especially after my grandmother loses her mind after my uncle is born. My grandmother tries to strangle a doctor at the hospital and they take her away to the insane asylum. In a few months she is better, but when she comes home and sees the little girl who is my mother, she screams. My mother runs away to her great-grandmother. Meanwhile, my father is hit on the head with a thrown-away baseball bat and nearly dies. His parents take him to Florida to recover.

The Second World War comes and goes. My grandparents take their families to the beach for the summer. This is how my parents meet. It is 1945, the summer of V-J Day. My father is eighteen, my mother thirteen. They fall in love. My father's friends kid him about such a young girlfriend, but he will not listen to them. In four years they are married. My mother has just graduated high school; my father has just dropped out of college. He will go into his father's business. They will take an apartment in Brooklyn. They will try to have a baby right away and they will not be able to have me until 1951.

(It is late Tuesday night and I am still typing. My mother is beginning to get worried. "Why do you have to take everything so seriously?" she asks me. I lock my bedroom door.)

Now of course the novel focuses on me. When my mother has one of her attacks of vertigo and leaves me alone on Utica Avenue, I panic. Luckily my grandmother happens to be walking by. It seems I am a bright child. I read the Almanac at three. I can read all the Golden Books already and I am bored with them. By five I know the capital of every state and nation. In kindergarten I don't cry on the first day but on the second day I throw up. I become nervous and refuse to carry the flag in assembly because my heart will beat so fast it will stop. I have few friends. I am overprotected. We move to a house, and I go to a new school. I am absent a lot. I have two more brothers. I don't grow very tall. I am skinny. I am a coward. I do very well in school. I have a lavish bar mitzvah, which I hate; in the morning my parents are counting the gifts and entering them into a notebook. I transfer out of my high school because I am afraid to take swimming. I go to private school. I begin having attacks of nausea. Everyone says this is just nerves. An aunt tells me I should see a psychiatrist. I just want to go back to a new public school. I refuse to go to summer camp. I am an outcast in high school. No one sits next to me in Honor English. I read psychology books and discover things about myself that are very strange. I begin to have anxiety attacks in school. I go to my aunt's psychiatrist. I am too nervous to go to my high school graduation. I do not go to college in the fall, but stay in my room for several months. I am nauseated all the time. I gradually take myself out of the house, go to college, see a new psychiatrist, become active in the antiwar movement, make a lot of friends, decide I am homosexual, have a girlfriend, fall in love, my girlfriend leaves me for my best friend, I cry a lot, I go to the 1972 Democratic National Convention as an alternate delegate, I fall in love with a friend of my old girlfriend who is now married, I change my major from Poli Sci to English, I win a playwrighting award, I become a big man on campus, I go to graduate school, I break up with my girlfriend, I stop going to therapy, I finally get part-time jobs delivering laundry and being a messenger and working in a department store, I go for an M.F.A. in Creative Writing, I try to be Henry James, I get a break when a teacher dies and I am called in to replace him and teach Freshman English, I gain weight, I lose weight, I don't get involved, I have crushes on male friends and platonic affairs with female friends, my old girlfriend's husband ironically turns out to be gay, my grandfather moves to Florida and dies, I continue to live in my parents' house and I continue to write short stories which are published in many little magazines and I continue to teach for a low salary and I continue to, continue to, continue to. . . .

It is by now Thursday afternoon. It is raining. I close my novel with this sentence:

He still believed in everything.

Then I fall asleep and have no dreams. When I wake up, a year and a half later, Houghton Mifflin (not Harper and Row) has published my novel. It has been reviewed favorably in the New York *Times* on the day of a power blackout when no one has read the paper. Still, the sales are not bad for a first novel. They go into a second printing. I get an offer to teach full-time. I move out of my parents' house and get my own apartment. I continue to write, to eat, to breathe, to whine, to snicker, to be bored, to be angry, to be cutting, to be mischievous, to be very frightened. One day I get a note from you telling me how much you liked my novel and I think that this makes it all worth it. I still believe in everything.

CROSS IN THE WATER

It was such a grey day. And cold, too—cold even for mid-January. There were flurries of snow which melted as soon as they touched the pier, which was also grey; the snow-flakes looked as if they were stationary in the air, hovering above the crowd which had gathered together for the ritual of Greek Cross Day.

Randy's teeth were chattering. He was only half-listening to Archbishop Kotteakos' speech, concentrating on keeping himself warm by sheer will alone. It didn't matter that it was seventeen degrees; his will should be stronger than any cold. He felt guilty about being up on the pier, so close to the Archbishop, at the head of the crowd. He knew he was not worthy.

Father Economou had laughed at Randy when the boy had come to his study late one afternoon the week before. "You want to decline in favor of Vasilatos?" the priest had repeated. "Are you questioning my good judgment, Chiragros? Suggesting that I reverse a decision already made? What's the matter Chiragros? Are you afraid to swim?"

"It's not that, Father," Randy had said, stammering; he had asked his uncle to allow him to come late to work and he had been thinking of all the dishes piling up in the sink of the restaurant's kitchen. "Then what *is* the matter, young man?" he heard the priest say to him. "It's a great honor—I would say a very great honor—to be selected to represent your school and your church at Greek Cross Day. . . . You know what the day is all about, don't you Periander?" Randy always winced when he was called by his given name; he didn't care that he was named, as his grandmother always reminded him, for the famous tyrant of Corinth. He wanted to be called Randy. When he got old enough, he would have his name changed legally.

He had told the priest he knew all about the Epiphany, and the visit of the Wise Men to Bethlehem, and Our Lord's first miracle at the wedding at Cana, and most importantly, of Christ's baptism by his cousin, St. John the Baptist, in the River Jordan. Randy could recite paragraphs from the textbook, verses from the Bible; he could even recall parts of Father Economou's lectures word for word. It had surprised him when he discovered that this was unusual, that everyone did not have what the schoolteacher had called "a photographic memory."

A photographic memory! That was the whole trouble. How could he, Randy Chiragros, be the one to retrieve the cross from the river? He kept seeing that picture of Lina, those breasts of hers, her face like that, the way she lay on that small half-covered table and parted her legs before him. . . .

The Archbishop was reading from the Bible, quoting a passage that Randy was not very familiar with: ". . . Let both grow together until the harvest; and in the time of harvest I will say to the reapers, Gather ye together first the tares, and bind them in bundles to burn them; but gather the wheat into my barn. . . . " Randy would make a good show of it—that he knew he had to do. It was like a fixed boxing match in all those movies. There was one with John Garfield, and one with Ricardo Montalban, and another one with somebody Randy did not know. Randy had not been in too many fights, but he had won, or nearly won, them all. Today he would make this look good. He would let one of the other boys get the cross. It wouldn't be right for him to be the one; not after Lina.

How could he tell Father Economou the real reason, the whole thing that happened with Lina? It was nearly a sin to even think about such things in the presence of a priest. Father Economou had picked Randy out of everyone in the school because Randy was the smartest; actually, he was the second smartest, but Peter Galifinakis, who was first, was asthmatic and anyone looking at him could see he was too frail for a dive in the river in January. Randy had come to the priest's study to plead a case for his withdrawal in favor of Spiro Vasilatos. Vasilatos was not that good in English or in history, but he was better than Randy at math; quadratic equations gave Randy so much trouble. Moreover, Vasilatos was a strong swimmer, a good two inches taller and ten pounds heavier than Randy. Randy had started working out with the weights his cousin had left behind when he went into the army, but he had only been at it for three months, and he had noticed the muscles in Vasilatos' upper arms and chest when they undressed for gym in the locker room.

Bodies. Why were they such strange things, always capable of surprising him? Even without any remembrance of Lina, there was a disturbance just the night before. To wake with the stickiness, the dampness—his grandmother wanted to know why he insisted on taking a shower that morning. "You'll get your dunking later, heaven knows," the old lady had said. He told her he wanted to make sure he was clean enough for the ceremony—there would be photographers sent from the newspaper—and his grandmother laughed and said, "Periander, you just want the girls to see you looking nice. I know all about boys." Was it true? Why then did she never mention the stains on the sheets? Perhaps her eyesight was fading.

Sometimes he tried to imagine his grandmother being young, and looking like Lina, having Lina's body—it seemed wicked to think things like that, he knew, but the thoughts, like the morning stains, persisted at the most inappropriate moments. He found himself wondering more than once about Father Economou's penis, and what the priest did when he was naked or in bed. Randy chastised himself severely for harboring such thoughts.

It was always so boring washing the dishes in his uncle's restaurant. The hot, sudsy water seemed to be a spawning ground for hallucinations of all kinds; that is why he never really noticed what he should have about Lina. It was like a Turkish bath in there, and Randy's athletic undershirt always stuck to him like moist tissue. That was where the thing with Lina started. That look she gave him that night, the night of the snowstorm when things were slow and there were no customers for Lina to wait on. But he should have paid more attention to Lina before; then he wouldn't have missed the clues.

She wore makeup and false eyelashes and drew an outline with black mascara completely around her eyes. Her hair was different colors; light blonde here, nearly brown there. She had a rip in her white waitress' uniform, by the shoulder seam it was, and that's where he first saw Lina's skin—the skin on the parts of a woman he had never seen before, except in the photographs of magazines that Vasilatos used to bring to school, for during study hall.

He knew it would be better for Vasilatos to replace him in the ceremonies; although Vasilatos boasted about his experiences with women, Randy knew that he had never had any. Vasilatos had gotten things mixed up, completely wrong—unless Lina was abnormal, or he himself was, which

[111]

he doubted. It had gone off all right; a little scared in the beginning, he had managed to rely on instinct and on Lina. She pulled him on top of her in the small cramped closet behind the kitchen, the closet where all the cleaning supplies were stored. She took off all her clothes except her stockings, and they were only black mesh so Randy could see through them. She had done it so fast Randy knew that she must have done it very often or at least practiced a lot. He was ready almost immediately and somehow she knew it and she brought him out of himself and onto her body and she guided him along, adjusting his rhythms to hers until that moment came—it was like being pulled out of yourself, even more so than when you did it alone. There was so much heavy breathing and noise, he was afraid that someone would find them. But his uncle and the others stayed out front, talking with old Nikos, the lone customer on that night of the snowstorm.

After some time, he had wanted to sound experienced and so he told Lina, "I think we came stimunanimously." And she laughed and said, "What?" and he repeated the word, "Stimunanimously." And Lina had her white waitress' uniform on again, and she laughed at his word and kissed him on the forehead like a little child, leaving him alone in the closet-room, his face reddening in the darkness.

A snowflake hit Randy's nose and melted immediately. He looked at Archbishop Kotteakos with his jewels and crown and scepter, and the thought came to him: did the Archbishop ever do that with a girl like Lina? And when the Archbishop introduced him along with the two other boys— "Periander Chiragros from St. Nicholas Orthodox Church on Fourteenth Street"—Randy could not meet the old man's gaze. He could not be the one to retrieve the cross, but he would make a good show of it so that he would not embarrass his classmates or Father Economou or his grandmother.

[112]

He tried to banish the picture of that night from his mind, but it was not easy for someone with a photographic memory.

Somehow he had stripped down to his undershirt and the powder blue swimming trunks under his pants. The other two boys had done the same; he had just followed their actions without conscious effort. I must concentrate, Randy told himself. He had to make it look as though he wanted more than anything to be the one to retrieve the cross. He couldn't let anyone suspect that he had done things he was ashamed of. After all, it was a holy day; the ceremony represented the first baptism, the baptism of the Savior. The Christmas season had ended for the others in the city, but this would mark the end of the Greek holidays. Randy knew that the Orthodox Church still used the Julian calendar, and they were nearly two weeks behind the Gregorian calendar, the one that was used for everything else in the world. He looked to see if he had remembered to take off his wristwatch, the Christmas present from his grandmother. He had; his wrist was bare. With Lina, he had not really taken off any-anything, but she had still made him feel naked.

The Archbishop, with a surprisingly quick gesture, tossed the small gold cross into the choppy waters off the pier. The boys on either side of him had already dived in; he had hesitated; that was the end.

But without any conscious direction—later he would think how much like that it was with Lina—Randy dove into the water and it didn't feel cold—just wet and dark—and he was thinking all along about how his teeth had stopped chattering even though he was nearly naked on such a cold January day in the river; he was thinking about that when all of a sudden he found himself out of the water, standing straight, soaking wet, on the crowded pier, holding a small gold cross in his left hand.

The next morning his grandmother awoke him out of a dream to show him the newspaper. There was a photograph of himself, in his undershirt and swimming trunks, smiling broadly, standing next to the Archbishop, who was also smiling. The Randy of the newspaper photograph was holding the cross aloft, apparently glowing with triumph.

He stared at the picture for several minutes, and then yawned and turned in his bed to look out the window. The new day was not as grey as the day before. The winter was almost over, or so it seemed.

EARLY WARNINGS

There were a lot of grandparents.

Slowly he figured out how it worked. Grandpa Ike and Grandma Bess were his father's parents. Grandpa Ike was small and compact, and smoked cigars and gave him money, and said, "So long—hoo long—ha long" when he left. Grandma Bess was sick a lot and he thought she might die but she didn't. She drove a car (once, up a one-way street the wrong way) and her face looked pinched in at the corners and he was sometimes afraid of her because he thought that she knew somehow that he didn't like her as much as he liked Grandma Shirley.

Grandma Shirley was his mother's mother and she was married to Grandpa Abe. They were young, but not as young as his parents. Grandma Shirley baked cinnamon cookies and let him eat them while they were hot. He slept over at their house sometimes, in the room that used to belong to his uncle. Grandpa Abe was famous for watching television; everybody knew that. He had his own chair, in the living room, and only he could sit in it. Grandpa Abe smoked a lot of cigarettes and his face turned purple when he coughed. He always told Michael how, when Michael was little, he had lifted him up and because of that he, Grandpa Abe, had a bad back that hurt him every morning when he got out of bed. But Grandpa Abe wasn't really angry; Michael could play with his pipe rack and look at old pictures of Grandpa Abe when he was younger and in some place called Manila. Michael wanted to know where Manila was; one day, when Grandpa Abe gave him a giant atlas, he tried to find it, but couldn't.

There was Grandpa Meyer, but he died right away. Michael didn't really care because he was afraid of Grandpa Meyer. He always seemed to be looking angry, like one of the animals he made fur coats from. Once when Michael was in his house, Grandpa Meyer pushed him away so that he could play with Michael's cousin Robbie. Grandpa Abe took Michael out of the house; he was angry at Grandpa Meyer. "To prefer a grandchild to a great-grandchild," he said. "It isn't right." After Grandpa Meyer died, Michael learned that he was Grandma Shirley's father, which didn't make sense because how come Grandpa Meyer was so so scary and Grandma Shirley was so nice.

Grandma Dora was married to Grandpa Meyer, but she wasn't Grandma Shirley's real mother although she called her Momma. Grandma Shirley had showed him a picture of her real mother. The Russian soldiers had come into their house and killed her, just like that. Everyone else was hiding, and the Russian soldiers couldn't find them so they weren't shot. Grandma Dora was pretty nice. After Grandpa Meyer died, she worked in a department store and moved from the big house into a basement.

Most of all Michael liked Bubbe Ita. She was very old and very fat and she would stay with him sometimes when his parents would go out. Even though she was old she wouldn't take the trolley to get to their house—she liked to walk, she said, and wouldn't take the money Michael's father would give her. She spoke Jewish a lot to him and finally he understood a lot of it but he forgot it all after she died. She was very sick with something very strange; for years Michael thought it was called rue de la paix but later he discovered that it was actually called tic de la rue. She lost all her hair and they had to put her on a plane to Canada, by herself, to see some doctor, but the doctor couldn't help her so she died. She had bubbe arms, big fat arms with lots of crinkles.

His mother left him once, on a shopping street. Later he found out it was because she was dizzy with his brother inside her stomach. He was very lucky, though, because Grandma Shirley just happened to be passing by and so she found him and then she found his mother, who wasn't feeling well, and Grandma Shirley took them both home.

He was driving with his Grandpa Ike and Grandma Bess one time and they passed a store that had white paint or paste all over its windows. Grandpa Ike said something about a store being 'mobbed' and Michael thought he meant that store. It took him a long time to learn that 'mobbed' did not mean windows smeared with white stuff.

He remembered being held up by the window. There were venetian blinds on top. He would watch the cars go by, some one way, some another. He didn't think he could fall out of the window so he didn't cry.

Across the street there was the vegetable man. He had a big house with grass, not just an apartment; there were flowers and plants in his yard. The man worked in his garden a lot. Once he gave Michael a tomato and asked him if he was a good boy. Years later Michael would learn that the man was Carlo Gambino, and he was supposed to be very bad.

He started to read a book called the Almanac. He learned how to read by himself. The first word he knew was "Tide," from the detergent box. A teacher who lived next door gave him school-books, but he liked the Almanac best. He found Manila on the map in the Almanac, and then he found it on the map in the Atlas that was almost as big as he

[117]

was. Manila was the capital of the Philippines because it had a star next to it; that meant it was the most important city. Michael liked capitals and countries, and he wondered why places like Trans-Jordan and Manchukuo were in the big Atlas but not in the Almanac, and why Germany was bigger in the Atlas. In the Atlas it said you could get a supplement after the war if you sent back a coupon but the war was over for a long time and no one had sent back the coupon. Michael wanted to but figured it was too late.

He was afraid of barbers and dentists. He would cry in the chair. But finally he began to like Sol, the barber; his father got his haircuts there too and in the back his mother and Grandma Shirley and Grandma Bess got their hair cut too, only it was for women and called a beauty parlor; that part of the store smelled terrible from the purple stuff the women put on their hair. Once his father took him to a dentist who said he was very good with children and that his father could leave Michael alone with him. Only the dentist wasn't good with children and he had Michael's head locked in his arms and was cursing at Michael until his father came in and rescued him; he had heard the screaming.

The first day of kindergarten he didn't cry although a lot of kids did and he figured you were really sort of supposed to. On television they showed you how people were supposed to act. Like when his mother was having a baby and he woke up in the morning and Grandma Shirley was there instead and said that his parents had gone to the hospital; Michael knew you were supposed to pace up and down, so that's what he did, pace up and down the kitchen and the front room until the telephone rang and they said he had a brother.

His brother shared Michael's room, but he slept in a crib. The floor of the room said Michael in script and he wondered how they would get his brother's name written on the floor, too, only they never did. His wallpaper had cowboys and Indians on it and Michael was afraid that at night they would come off the wallpaper and shoot him. Once he thought he saw a wolf at the window at night, but everyone told him it was just a dream.

The kindergarten teacher wanted them to finish their milk so they could make a project with the empty milk container. Michael never finished his milk but that day he was afraid not to, even though he didn't want to. Walking by the playhouse, he got sick and suddenly there was vomit all over the classroom floor. It was terrible. But when he got out of school he told his mother that he had thrown up, just like it was nothing. Still, it bothered him, that people could vomit just like that—in school, anywhere.

The kindergarten teacher went away in the spring, and the other teacher, the younger one, took over the class. They said that the old teacher was away but Michael knew that she had died. They could fool the other kids but not him. At least he thought so until many years later when Michael had a date with a girl and she mentioned that she had had the old teacher for kindergarten two years after Michael did.

He was small and had trouble walking up and down stairs. In school they wanted you to do it first one leg on one one step, then the other leg on the next step. It was easier for him the other way, one foot and then the other on the same step, but Michael practiced doing it the way they wanted him to. When he was in fourth grade, a boy in his class would tell him that the boy's mother had been the younger kindergarten teacher and she said he didn't know how to walk up and down stairs and made the class slow on fire drills; the guys in fourth grade teased him about that.

Once his Grandpa Abe was watching a television show that showed the human heart—the real heart, beating, It frightened Michael terribly, that he had that inside of him.

He kept checking to see that his heart was still beating. If it ever stopped beating you were dead. In first grade one day, they had camphor in the classroom, camphor in water, and the teacher put it on his desk and he jumped up, scared. He had heard you could suffocate from camphor. The teacher said he was a baby and put the camphor on Benjamin's desk and said, "See *he* isn't afraid." Benjamin was the second smartest in the class, after Michael. They read books in first grade that Michael had read when he was little.

People found out he was good at capitals and people tried to stump him. When his Grandma Bess was in the hospital, he sat alone downstairs in the waiting room and a bald man he was talking to asked him what the capital of Cambodia was. "Phnom Penh," Michael said, although he wasn't sure he was pronouncing it right. "You're pretty good," the bald man said. Grandpa Abe wrote away to have him on a television program called "Take A Giant Step" but the program went off the air before everything was setttled. In a way, Michael was glad, because going on television would have made him nervous.

Once they went up to the country. Grandpa Abe told his father how to get there—he said to turn right at the sign for Brown's, the sign with Jerry Lewis saying "Brown's is my favorite resort." Except when they got to the sign there was a mountain to the right; if you turned you would crash into it. Michael thought they might get lost but they didn't, and for years afterward everyone would laugh when anyone said, "Turn right at Brown's." On the way home from the country, Michael went home with Grandma Shirley and Grandpa Abe, who drove very fast. They stopped at a diner and the woman behind the counter stumped Michael, or at least she thought she did. She said, "Name the capital of Kashmir," and Michael didn't know it but he didn't think it was a fair question since Kashmir wasn't really a country and

[120]

was striped on the map.

The principal of his school took him out of kindergarten one day. Michael sat down at a desk with a boy from sixth grade. They had a contest: the principal would say a country and they had to name the capital. They were even until the principal said "Taiwan" and Michael said "Taipei" first and won. When he came home his mother didn't believe him until a girl from down the block, who was in sixth grade, said that it was true.

Once he heard the old teacher in kindergarten talk about him. She whispered to the younger teacher that he had been absent seventy-five times. He knew it. But he didn't like school; they did dumb things. At home he could look at maps and read the Almanac and watch television and be with his mother and little brother. One time his mother didn't believe him when he said he was sick in the morning, and it turned out that he had the measles. Michael figured his mother was afraid of that happening again.

Grandma Bess said a funny thing once, that her stomach turned. He imagined his own stomach turning and thought how painful it must be. When his baby brother got sick it was very bad; he couldn't breathe and had asthma, and Michael was afraid it was because when they were painting the apartment he had smeared his brother's face with paint, just as a joke to make him look like a little clown. But he had put paint on his own face too and he wasn't sick with asthma. The doctor said his brother would have to go to the hospital and Grandma Bess came over to drive them there while Grandma Shirley stayed home with him and cried. She cried more than anybody he knew. She cried once when Grandpa Abe lost his job at the ladies' underwear factory; then Grandma Dora said, "Que sera, sera," and Grandma Shirley stopped crying. He thought it was magic. In eighth grade, when he studied the future tense, he finally understood the words were Spanish, even though he'd heard the song a lot of times since.

People said he was nervous, and he knew it too. Like when it was his turn in first grade to be the flag-bearer in assembly color guard, he was scared to go on stage. He didn't want to do it and the other kids told the substitute teacher, "He's nervous," and she said he didn't have to do it; when he got into second grade, the substitute teacher said, he wouldn't be so nervous. Michael was afraid he was too little to hold the flag up anyway. When he got nervous, his hands got all blotchy.

He and his brother ate a lot of St. Joseph's aspirin one day. They crawled up to the medicine chest and got it. They were orange-flavored and tasted good. He didn't get sick but his brother did because he was littler and his body couldn't take that many. The doctor told his mother to give his brother Liquiprin, which Michael thought strange. It was aspirin too, he knew, so how could that help?

He wasn't always scared. When he went for a tonsillectomy, he acted brave. There was a girl in the next bed, she was twelve years old, and she was carrying on. The doctor came in and said to her, "Look at this little boy, he isn't crying. Aren't you ashamed, at your age?" Afterwards he felt terrible and kept wanting to go home right away. His parents were there but they wouldn't take him home until the doctor said it was all right.

In first grade he had to have gas again, to have his teeth worked on. He was still afraid of dentists, so they said they could do it all while he was asleep. His teacher, who said she was married to a dentist, couldn't understand it and said, "Make sure you come to class that afternoon. Don't spoil our attendance record." But his mother said he'd be too groggy. Going under, they told him to count from one hundred backwards and when he got to ninety-three was dreaming. He dreamed he was on a stretcher being wheeled places, like it was a carnival ride or a tunnel of love. When he woke up, his teeth were all fixed and his parents had his present—a toy car dashboard.

Michael took Lady with him places. She was a stuffed poodle a man had given him when he was born. One time he left Lady in a laundromat by accident and Grandma Bess and Grandma Shirley had to go back to get her. Later on he didn't need Lady anymore. He was getting older.

His parents bought a house. He would watch it being built and even go in it before it was finished. He liked the smell of the building. It would be their own house, and he'd have a backyard, and go to a new school.

He went with another girl and her mother to register at the new school. They were moving in next door to Michael's family. Michael said he was nervous when he went to the new school and the girl's mother told him, "Children don't get nervous. They just get jumpy."

They moved over the summer. The first week of second grade, he waited outside to go into the auditorium for lunch. This was an eighth grade school, not a sixth grade school, and some of the kids were really big. Michael was still very short. The doors leading to the auditorium opened and everyone started pushing and shoving to get in as fast as possible. They were really in a rush—it was scary. He got knocked down to the ground and people started walking over him. He felt people stepping on his back, hard. No one seemed to notice. He thought he was going to die and envisioned his grave and people talking about "the late Michael Tate." He couldn't breathe. There was a blank. Finally, somehow it ended. He didn't cry. A kid from seventh grade helped him up and into the auditorium and shared his lunch with him because Michael's was lost. He was a nice big kid; he was blond and had freckles and blue veins up and down his arms and he kept

asking Michael if he was all right.
Michael said that he was.

DOUGLAS, APROPOS OF NOTHING

However

When he entered high school he was supposed to take swimming. You had to pass swimming to get out of a city high school. The boys swam nude. The day before their first swimming class the redheaded man who was to be their teacher tried to allay their apprehensions: "Some of you are big and some of you are small. Some of you are smooth and some of you are hairy. But the only thing you should be concerned with is learning to swim."

Douglas, after a week of not learning how to swim, told his mother that he felt stifled in the city school and that he wanted to go to a private school which could prepare him better for college. His mother had him transferred to a school where everyone wore blue blazers and white shirts except on every other Friday, Human Day, when they could wear anything they wanted while their school jackets were being dry-cleaned.

The first day in the new school was a drizzly October day. Sitting by the Scottish principal's desk, Douglas looked out the window at the park and felt himself feeling comfortable.

[125]

But then the principal, who had contracted a case of malaria in the first World War, told him: "Meeting a new class is the scariest experience you'll ever have." Then Douglas began to feel anxious. His tie was too tight around his neck.

The principal assigned a boy named George Bradley Schweitzer to take Douglas down to meet his new class. They were in History, studying the Punic Wars. In the city schools they never taught anything like that.

Douglas' father used to leave him off at the bus stop on Eighth Avenue and Fourteenth Street to catch the bus uptown to school. Douglas stood under the awning of a Spanish restaurant mornings, and when the bus did come he always sat on the right side so he could look out that window. On Fifty-first Street George and his stepbrother got on the bus; it was almost always the same bus as Douglas'. Sometimes, if Douglas' father had dropped him off too early, Douglas would let one or two buses go by so he could be on the same one with George. George's stepbrother went to a different private school, a progressive one where they could wear jeans and long hair. When people started wearing longer Beatle-like hair in Douglas and George's school, the principal got on the public address system and told the students he would not tolerate "asinine imitations of famous people."

George and Douglas became friends although they never saw each other outside of school except on the bus. George's stepfather was a television news producer and gave George photos of actors and actresses that he showed to Douglas. George himself got to play a boy with appendicitis on the CBS *National Health Quiz*. They shot the scene in somebody's mansion in Eastchester. George gave Douglas a copy of the script to read and when the show went on, Douglas thought George was really convincing and a good actor.

George had an attache case, a brown one with his initials on it: GBS, like George Bernard Shaw. Douglas got himself an attache case too, brown but without his initials, which were DOG and embarrassing.

One day in the locker room while they were dressing for gym George got into a fight with another boy, who socked him hard in the jaw. George went down and Douglas, putting on his gym shorts by his locker, wondered if he should go over to George but decided not to. Nobody else did. In gym, when they were lined up, Douglas craned his neck and saw the redness on the left side of George's jaw. But he never said anything about it to him. Douglas didn't get into fights; he didn't have a temper.

George couldn't take tests well. He was very bright but he froze up on tests, especially standardized ones. He only scored in the 26th percentile on the PSAT and did even worse on the NMSQT. Douglas was in the 98th percentile in the PSAT and got a letter of commendation for his achievement on the NMSQT. "I'm just not a standardized test taker," George would tell Douglas as they were putting relish on their hamburgers at lunch, and Douglas would nod his head.

Once Douglas stayed out of school for two weeks because he hated it so and George sent him a get-well card. It made Douglas feel guilty. Finally his parents forced Douglas to go back to school and when George asked him what the matter was, Douglas stepped over his attache case and said, "I just got over the grip."

The next year Douglas went to a different school and his friendship with George, if it was a friendship, was over.

Moreover

Douglas read in the new school library's *Encyclopedia Judaica*: "Whereas the more liberal attitude found in some modern Christian circles is possibly due to the exaggerated importance Christians have traditionally placed upon the term 'love,' Jewish law holds that no hedonistic ethic, even if called 'love,' can justify the morality of homosexuality."

Douglas cracked his knuckles.

Consequently

Shira was an Orthodox Jewish girl at the new school who became his best friend. He told her everything, all of it. She had secrets of her own. She liked to read a German poet, and she had to have Douglas take his books out of the library because her parents would not approve of anything German. Shira went over to Douglas' house and read her German poet there.

"Listen to this," Shira said one day as they lay on his bedroom floor. " 'Love consists in this, that two solitudes protect and touch and greet each other.' "

Douglas lay on his stomach, not saying anything.
Then Shira said, "What do you think?"
He looked up. "It's true."
She nodded.

Then his mother knocked and said she thought it would be better if Douglas kept his door open while Shira was in his bedroom with him.

They opened the door and laughed themselves into oblivion.

Still

The summer after graduation Shira went with her mother to Israel. She and Douglas exchanged long letters; he ended his, "Your obedient savant, Douglas," and she ended hers, "Don't do anything I wouldn't do, Shira."

Going back to America, Shira's TWA plane was hijacked by representatives of the Popular Front for the Liberation of Palestine. Shira wasn't afraid at first; she couldn't get over the feeling that it was only a joke.

But as the six days on the Jordanian desert dragged on, Shira's face broke out into a terrible rash. She never cried once but it was so hard when there were only bananas to eat. She started writing long letters to Douglas but the hijackers wouldn't let her finish them. Then they made her open her wallet and they looked at what she had in it. They took Douglas' high school graduation photo from her, and they questioned her insistently about the photo of the young Israeli soldier she had met. The Palestinians even took away the tape of a summer jazz concert.

Shira's mother was very brave and set up a kind of kindergarten for the seven little children on the plane. Shira found herself listening to her mother's fairy tales to the children, aware that she had never known that woman in quite that way. Shira composed a song for the children, to the tune of "Blowin' in the Wind":

> How many days must we stay on the plane
> Before we are left to go free?
> How many years must countries be at war
> Before they can all be friendly? . . .

The little children liked Shira's singing.

Finally they all watched in horror as the plane was wired with explosives. But the hijackers said they would be taken off before the plane was blown up. Shira and some other American girls were in the last bus convoy to leave. Their Palestinian driver drove a short distance away, then stopped to watch the plane blow up. He was excited about it, even joking. A large chunk of burning plane narrowly missed hitting Shira.

When she was back in the States, Shira told Douglas about her ordeal and he hugged her tightly. She mentioned that the hijacker had taken his photo away.

"He probably thought I was cute," Douglas told her. "Even Palestinians do it, I hear."

Similarly

Actually he could never bring himself to believe that anyone on earth really had sex except for himself and the people he had sex with.

Meanwhile

Douglas and his father were eating sunflower seeds and watching "Casablanca" on the floor of his parents' bedroom. At a commercial Douglas' father turned to him and said, "You should find yourself a girlfriend."

It was the first time he had ever said that to Douglas but Douglas knew that it had cost his father a great effort.

"A girlfriend?" Douglas said, stuffing a handful of sunflower seeds in his mouth and then chewing. "What would I do with one?"

His father said nothing, just went back to watching Humphrey Bogart and Ingrid Bergman.

Also

Later Douglas would call it "breaking the fuck barrier": He would say the word *fuck* in front of his parents when he got angry and his father would beat him for it. The sound of the word enraged his normally quiet father and turned him into a rabid dog. But Douglas kept using the word week in and week out and finally his father didn't lift a finger to stop him. His mother didn't even say "That's not how we talk" anymore.

After he could get away with *fuck*, he tried cancer. At the dinner table with his parents and younger brother, he would say, "They say one out of every four people gets cancer. Which one of us do you think will get it?" Nobody liked this kind of talk, of course.

The family hated it when he said, "Let's play a game. Which one of us do you think is going to die first, and what do you think he's going to die from?" But they couldn't stop Douglas from talking. Nobody could.

Furthermore

He wrote in the spiral notebook:
"To get away for a day—a vacation. Isn't this nice, I think. I'm really close by home, but knowing I won't have to go back to that house tonight makes me feel so free. I'm feeling good. Sexy. The first thing I did after getting into the room and checking out the typical Holiday Inn decor—rather nice if bland—was to draw the shades and take off my shirt and look at myself before the full-length mirror. I was surprised at my own body. I never seem to look this good in the mirrors at home. I have a *great* body. Why have I never realized it before? I flexed my muscles for a couple of minutes and then, feeling slightly silly and a bit cold, put back on my shirt. I actually would like to get someone into bed here tonight. For the first time I would take *anyone*—male or female, young or old, it doesn't matter—just as long as the body is warm. This motel room is *mine*. Old Virginia Woolf was right. I hear the cars going by on the highway. The maids are making up the other rooms. My door lets out to the outside, to the elevator and the soda machine, and I feel terrific. I don't know what to do with my freedom, however.

"What is it that has made me remain a child? Surely my case is not unique in the annals of blah, blah, blah. Oh hell. I hear voices. Teenage boys, I think. I am not more than a teenage boy myself. I would like to lure them in here and

[132]

suck their cocks. They are whistling and starting up their car now. One is calling out, 'Hey, Mommy! Are you ready?'

"More voices. Oh, pipes shaking. I feel like I have been here my whole adult life. *This may be true.*

"I remember seeing some actress on the Mike Douglas show once. Primal therapy had changed her whole life, she said, and it all started when they locked her into a motel room all by herself. Ain't life funny that way?"

Nevertheless

It was 1977. He was in an entirely different city. Douglas was a lawyer with Legal Aid. At the office they called him "Young RFK." He had shaved off his beard.

He was at a party. The hostess was another Legal Aid lawyer who reminded him so much of Shira. Shira was living in Israel now; she had a doctor husband and twins. There were too many people in the room, and too much smoke, but Douglas was smiling.

He got into a discussion with a woman his own age, a strikingly beautiful woman. She was talking about the conviction of Larry Flynt, the publisher of·*Hustler*, on obscenity charges. The woman was glad of this: "Have you ever seen *Hustler*? It's pure filth."

No, he had never seen *Hustler* and he had no interest in doing so. But the First Amendment was the First Amendment, for marching Nazis, for ex-radicals like themselves, even for pornographers like Flynt. Douglas tried to argue with her rationally, but she ended the discussion by saying:

"Well, I can talk to you from today till tomorrow and you'll never understand—because you have a penis instead of a vagina."

Douglas was taken aback: "What can I say to that?" So he smiled and made his way across the room. The stereo was playing Carly Simon singing "I Haven't Got Time for the Pain." He nodded at a couple of friends by the couch and then he saw someone waving to him from the corner. The man looked amazingly like an older George Bradley Schweitzer.

In Other Words

"Elvis is dead," said the television, "but you can share his legacy simply by sending $6.99 for the records and $8.99 for the eight-track tapes . . . ."

In front of the set Douglas wasn't watching or listening. He was too damn happy for anything like that.

REFLECTIONS ON A VILLAGE ROSH HASHONA 1969

Somebody like Pete Hamill or Norman Podhoretz or Gloria
Steinem once observed that one of the longest journeys in the
world is the trip from Brooklyn to Manhattan. I made that
trip last Rosh Hashona on the D train, which is a very good
train as far as they go. It was one of the last really warm days
of the summer and I dreaded staying home doing nothing but
playing solitaire or watching soap operas.

Actually, I used to be a soap opera addict, and still get the
urge to turn them on when I'm at home during the day. My
friend Jerry and I used to rush home from junior high to
catch the last fifteen minutes of "Another World" almost
every day. The best actress on the program played Aunt Liz,
and I truly hated her. The last time I saw Jerry, he told me a
new actress was playing Aunt Liz now, and she's not half as
evil.

During the 1964 World's Fair, Jerry and I went into this exhibit of some little jerkwater religion whose name I don't
remember. The man in charge of the exhibit was trying to
convert people, and when he found out we were Jewish, he
went into a long harangue about Jews having animal
sacrifices. I don't remember much of what he said. I wanted

to get Jerry out of there. Hell, he never was bar-mitzvahed
and in another ten minutes he would have converted. I keep
remembering what the man yelled at us as we walked away:
"But where's the blood, fellas? Where's the blood?!"

I started in psychoanalysis in the fall of 1966. If you remember, that was the time when Rockefeller had all those cute
commercials for his reelection. He could afford it, I guess.
One of them was about a talking fish. Not that I'm saying
that that had any connection with my seeing a shrink; it may
be a coincidence. Dr. Weinberg had his office in his big
mansion on Albemarle Road, and it smelled of jasmine.
When Arlene gives me a cup of jasmine tea, I remember Dr.
Weinberg.

The year before that, I enrolled as a sophomore at The
Benton School, which caters to upper-middle class Jews. It
was a long trip from Brooklyn to the Upper West Side, but I
always arrived early, even in the winter. Sometimes I arrived
before the registrar, Mrs. Mogg, who opened up the school.
It got very cold in the mornings, and I would stay in a telephone booth. Incidentally, on all of Central Park West, I
never found a telephone that worked.
        The principal of the school, an Englishman who occa-
sionally took a nip of brandy for the malaria he contracted
in the First World War, told me on the first day that he
would assign an older student to look after me for awhile.
He told me not to depend on this one student. The student's
name was Peter. His stepfather was the anchorman for the
six o'clock news.

Some time later, I put an ad in *The Village Voice*. I don't
remember it word for word, but it was good, like a prose
poem. I asked for a friendly guy or girl to share a trip around

New England. I got a lot of replies, mostly from weirdos or old people. When I read Erik's letter, I knew he was the right one.

First we went to New Haven. I didn't like Yale, probably because it wasn't what I expected. I expected some elegance. All I got was noise, crowds and confusion. Sometimes I think I should have been born in the nineteenth century. I'm a Victorian at heart.

I heard a cute story about my little next-door neighbor's first day in nursery school. The teacher put up one finger and asked the kid what it was, and the kid answered, "One." Then the teacher held up two fingers and asked what it was. The kid answered, "Peace."

Last Rosh Hashona was the fifth time that I had gone into Manhattan that year. Once I went to a dental laboratory to pick out a shade for my capped tooth, the one I broke in the obstacle race in Jerry's basement. Once I went to visit a friend who works at Barnes and Noble. Twice I went to the Village, to Washington Square. That's also where I went last Rosh Hashona.

Did you ever notice that the West Fourth Street station of the IND has entrances on Sixth Avenue, West Eighth Street and Waverly Place, but no entrance on West Fourth Street? Avis loves to hear about things like that. I had received a letter from Avis that very morning.

Dear Michael,
This has been a momentous day, and I celebrate it with this letter. Two of my friends and I (hard core hoodlums all) were invited to leave French class for the next two weeks. The teacher thought she was threatening us, but we plan to

take her up on it. We were accused of "disrupting the class, disrespectful behavior, inattention" blah blah blah. What really happened was that I questioned her translations and teachings, Pat broke into laughter when asked to translate, and Cris stuck up for us. Cris is overly sensitive and almost broke into tears under the tongue-lashing she received.

Speaking of trouble, there have been four or five fire bombings around the University. They bombed the wrong side of the gymnasium so that the only thing that remained unscathed was the ROTC offices. Although these people are rather inept, I sympathize with them. I'd really like to burn down West, tho, and then the University. I don't dare say that at home.

I'd like to grow all my own foods, grind the grain, dye and weave the cloth, use the sun and wind for power; in short, be more self-sufficient. Speaking of handicrafts (writing of them, actually) Cris and I are selling macrame belts at a local store. I made a blue belt for you, but either I measured wrong or it shrank in the dye, because it came out three inches too short. So I sold it. But abandon not hope, I'll try again. I'll knot be defeated.

Dr. Conigliaro has been playing with my hair again. He's always telling me what a good wife I'll make some lucky man. Yesterday he was muttering about how he'd like to 'get first crack' at me.

The Cream record is ending, so so long for now.

Love, Avis

It was in September of 1968 that I had a nervous breakdown. I didn't sleep for three nights and I fainted. I had chills and nausea for hours. I shook and shook and shook. I couldn't do anything, I couldn't leave my house. I was even scared to go down to the basement. It was as though my nerves were sticking out, as though my flesh had been torn away. My physician prescribed Librium and a hot bath. My shrink prescribed Valium and group therapy.

I was totally recovered by last Rosh Hashona. I bought a magazine—I believe it was *Ramparts*—and strolled over to Washington Square to sit in the sun by the fountain. Next to me, perched on one of the pedestals, was a young kid, maybe sixteen. His dark brown hair fluttered over his eyes. He was wearing an old work shirt, black dungarees with the name "Diann" written vertically on the right leg with white paint, and very abused brown loafers, no socks. I squinted through my shades, trying to see his face. He had a large nose, the kind that kids around that age get when their noses grow faster than the rest of them. He was squinting himself, at the whole scene, as if he were reviewing it for a magazine. Outasight. He looked a little like Peter.

I was fourteen, Peter was sixteen, and we were in the bathroom of his East Side apartment. I started to feel a bit funny, as though I were being torn apart from myself, and pulled away, but Peter drew me closer. "Nothing's happening," I heard myself say. Soon enough though, persistence paid off and I gasped, "Christ!" Like a meteor being drawn to earth by gravity. I fell toward Peter's long smooth body and exploded. After about a century, Peter smiled and said, "Great. But listen, could you try and be a little neater next time, huh?"

    Peter's mother committed suicide last year. It made page three of the *Post*. I thought of sending a sympathy card, but decided against it.

A bearded man in his forties came over to the kid in Washington Square, and started asking him all kinds of questions. From time to time, I could make out snatches of the conversation. The kid said that he was in from Minnesota to be at his mother's wedding. "What if your new stepfather takes a liking to you? You know what I mean?" said the dirty old man. "I'm not going to live with my stepfather," the kid announced. "I'm staying with my aunt at her motel in Hibbing." He spoke with a very broad A. The man started talking about himself: he was a science fiction writer and wanted the kid to come up to his nearby studio and see his collection of flying saucer photos. By this time, the kid kept looking at me for something, and the man noticed this. "Are you his boyfriend?" the man asked me. I smiled, looked at the kid, who nodded, and said, "Yes. Yes, I am. And if you'll please leave us alone." The man snapped his fingers like a movie villain and went on to the next young boy.

"Thanks," the kid said. "He was getting to be a drag."

"You don't know how to handle these dirty old men. But I guess you don't get much of that sort of thing in Minnesota."

He brightened tremendously, and said, "You believed that story? I made the whole thing up. I'm from Brooklyn. Brooklyn Heights."

Dumbfounded, I could only manage to say, "I'm from Brooklyn, too." We talked for a while. I told him my name.

He was Jack Krantz, born in Tennessee, but moved here when he was a baby. His father was a surgeon, his mother a pop artist. He went to Poly Prep, and was fifteen. He was waiting for his seventeen-year-old sister.

I didn't get much out of group therapy, mostly because I was more interested in the other patients than I was in myself. One girl was a heroin addict who was going cold turkey, and she was awfully fidgety. One girl was having two love affairs at once: she liked both guys and it became a hassle

after a while. One guy stabbed his mother. He lived next
door to Dr. Weinberg, and I guess the good doctor took him
on as a favor to his neighbors. One girl was pregnant and not
married. She had been molested by her grandfather and told
some of the greatest jokes I've ever heard. I never did find
out what was the matter with the last guy, mainly because
he never said anything. Oh, sometimes Dr. Weinberg would
try and ask him something, but he always said, "Talking
makes me nervous." Which is the opposite of me. I can go
on and on, and usually do.

Jack's sister was named Arlene. He introduced me to her
when she arrived, and they invited me to wander around the
Village with them. Arlene was blonde, with freckles; skinny
but well-built. She was very bright. I inferred this when she
asked me what I majored in. I told her I wasn't sure now but
that last term I was an English major. "Really?" she asked.
"What regiment?" I think it was then that I started to fall
in love with Arlene.
    It was the nicest Rosh Hashona I can remember. The
three of us watching the kooks and the tourists, ate bad
pizza (which I paid for, happily), shopped in all the stores
(but didn't buy a thing), and generally joked around. We
were on West Eighth Street, by Orange Julius, and I looked at
my watch and said, "Gee, you guys. It's been great, but I
really have got to get going.' Hey, do you mind if I call you?"
    "Our number's in the book," Arlene answered. "Mrs.
Sheera Krantz. Nineteen Grace Court." She gave my
shoulder a squeeze. "See you soon."
    I didn't sleep at all that night.

Erik and I visited his cousin in Toronto. His cousin was an
old maiden lady, who would be played by Margaret Ruther-
ford if they ever did her life story. Her name was Shifra, and

she didn't mind that we called her by her first name. We got to discussing cities and their names, and she told us how to spell Chicago: "Chicken in the car, car won't go, that's how you spell Chicago." She also recited a poem for us:

> *I won't go to Macy's any more, more, more.*
> *There's a big fat policeman at the door, door, door.*
> *He'll squeeze you like a lemon,*
> *A kalatchgazolenemon.*
> *I won't go to Macy's any more.*

Arlene says the poem would make a good ad for A & S.

I not only spent Rosh Hashona with Jack and Arlene, but Yom Kippur, too. I found their apartment in Brooklyn Heights after great difficulty, and their mother made us grilled cheese sandwiches. They were open sandwiches, with tomatoes, and were very good. Then we went back to the Village, but I guess you can't go home again, and it wasn't as much fun on Yom Kippur as it was the time before. We did a lot of things that fall. I would wait for Arlene when she came out of school (Packer Collegiate) and we would go to Coney Island or the Cloisters or Bethesda Fountain, sometimes with Jack, sometimes just the two of us. By November and Lindsay's re-election, Arlene was my girl.

My father likes to tell the story of the first time I ate Chinese food. My mother asked me how I liked the chow mein. I said, "I like the chow but not the mein." I also had a stuffed lamb that I called Lambie Pie. There was a music box inside the lamb. When you wound it up, it played, "Mary Had a Little Lamb." It still works.

Jack and Dr. and Mrs. Krantz had gone out to visit Dr.

Krantz's grandmother, who was about a zillion years old. Arlene and I were in her house, watching "The Forsyte Saga." It was the episode in which Soames rapes Irene. Arlene and I made love during the show. I felt so secure inside of her that I never wanted to leave. To prolong it, I thought of the starving Biafran children. I came anyway. A few minutes after it was all over and Arlene lit a cigarette, I began to feel hungrier than I ever did in my life. I drank a whole quart of skim milk and ate four slices of toast with cherry jelly. An hour later, I threw it all up on the Clark Street subway tracks.

You know what I like most about Arlene? Her veins. She has beautiful purple veins flowing through her breasts. They remind me of the canals of Mars.

The movies that Arlene and I have seen lately all have definite endings: *Easy Rider, Midnight Cowboy, Medium Cool.* It's almost Rosh Hashona again, and I can't think up an ending. It's like that delicatessen in Rockaway with mirrors on each wall. You see your reflection, and your reflection in your reflection, and so on. There's a guy I know at school. Everytime I meet him, he tells me that tomorrow's the end of the world. One of these days he's going to be right.

I, ELIZA CUSTIS

June 4, 1831

I take the pen to write a narrative of my life, from my earliest recollection to this time. However deficient my story may be in other respects, it shall have the merits of truth and candor. I wish not to appear better than I am—but justice to myself imperiously calls upon me to tell the story of a life which, although not a very long one, has been marked by events of no common order. The world knows nothing of me, and it may possibly continue in ignorance. But I feel it is important to me, having passed the age of fifty, to recount the events of my life for those who may wish in the future to know the full story of my existence upon this planet.

It has been said of me that I have loved the world and its admiration too greatly. I do not think this is possible. I was born in August of 1776, making me but one month younger than the nation I have lived in for over fifty years, and I have loved this nation, and I suppose I have been loved as well. Still, I have been unable to successfully conclude the quest that I started so long ago, and I wish to go on living for a long time. But this, I fear, is not meant to be; I feel a shadow over my bed each night when I retire, and I wonder just how much time is left for me. Hence this narrative.

The family from which I am a descendant was among the first settlers of Virginia. I do not know exactly from where they came, but I think I recollect being told they were from some part of Flanders—this may be a mistake, but it is not material. They possessed wealth at the time of their establishment, and by good management became proprietors of some of the most valuable land on the eastern shore and lower counties of the state which they inhabited. I have always felt pride in hearing that all who had borne the name of Custis were honest and just men, a circumstance more to be prized in the opinion of their descendants than all the pomp of wealth or heraldry could give. The father of my father was a good man. Possessed of a great estate and himself a pleasing man of unblemished reputation, he at an advanced age married Miss Dandridge, to whom in her infancy he had been godfather. In his youth my grandfather often dandled on his knee the smiling cherub who was to become one day his wife, and afterwards the wife of General Washington.

Mr. Custis made a most affectionate and indulgent husband to the most charming woman of the age. Four children were the pledges of their union—two of them died in infancy, and the loss of his oldest son so preyed upon the soul of my grandfather that he pined away, his other blessings unable to dissipate his melancholy, and he sank into the grave, leaving his youthful widow with a large dowry and a lovely girl and boy to engage those affections he had shared with them. My grandmother was worth all of the praise which her virtues obtained from all who ever knew her, and after a period of mourning in which her correct conduct added to the esteem in which she had been held, she was selected by Washington to be the partner of his happiness and his country's love—the companion in a life of glory. Well did she repay his confidence and attachment. O ever-honored spirit of my grandmother, look down upon me! How little did your fond heart think, when caressing your darling Eliza, that I would one day be the victim of slander and persecution, and, with a heart lacerated by the ravages of a neglected and loveless life, would now commence a narrative of my life to convince the world of the purity of my soul and the constant rectitude of my intentions.

With the hand of Mrs. Custis, General Washington received a large fortune and became the guardian of her son and daughter. They removed to Mount Vernon, where he procured a tutor to instruct the children and where his wife garnered the admiration of all who saw her. The general was attentive to her children and desirous of giving my father every advantage. He placed the boy, Jacky—the handsomest youth of the day—in a school run by Parson Boucher. At the age of sixteen, my father became acquainted with the family of Mr. Calvert of Maryland, and he soon fell desperately in love with my mother—then only fourteen, she was as beautiful as an angel. My father saw her just once, and he was in love with her for his whole life. However, he was but a boy, and although his heart was accepted by my mother, and her family exulted in her conquest, it was thought best to insist upon his going to New York to acquire some sort of education. My grandparents and aunt visited Miss Calvert and were highly delighted with the proposed marriage, but they desired her to influence Jacky to attend to those studies necessary to complete his education. After much consultation with his family, my father decided to go to New York, feeling much reluctance to leave my mother but desirous of making himself even more worthy of her.

I now leave my father in New York, to which place General Washington accompanied him, and return to Mount Vernon, where my mother had gone to spend some time. The sister of my father was an amiable girl, dutiful to her parents, adoring of her brother, and much attached to his intended wife. My aunt suffered from bad health, and one day she was sitting with her mother, talking of their beloved Jacky, when she fell to the floor with a moan. My mother, having heard the noise, put her to bed; my grandmother, frantic, ran about seeking assistance; and the godlike man who afterwards saved his country kneeled by the bedside, solemnly reciting the prayers for the dead while tears rolled down his cheeks.

The Angel of Death hovered over and snatched his prey from the family. Deprived of one darling child, my Grandmother Washington sent for my father to console her. My father's faith was unchanged by his absence, and he brought back a heart uncontaminated by intercourse with a world of which he was the most brilliant ornament. Many efforts had been made by New York ladies to supplant the woman he loved, but these all proved to be of no avail. Being of a respectable family and a large fortune, and a person as beautiful as the love of God, the young Virginian found that many mothers sought to engage his attentions on their daughters, and many a lovely girl attempted to captivate him. But his heart was fixed and incapable of perfidy and desertion (would that I had known such a lover!) and he came back if possible more devoted to his Eleanor than when they parted. He swore he would not leave her again and wished them to be married at once, but his impetuosity was controlled so that he was kept single till the age of nineteen. When he reached that age, my father and my mother, she not yet sixteen, were united. I have been told that when arrayed in white, which was the fashion of the day, and standing in the midst of their numerous guests to receive the nuptial benediction, they looked as if some inhabitants of heaven had descended to gladden the children of earth. He was the most ardent lover, the most enraptured husband—he loved his wife to excess and thought there was no heaven except in her arms.

They resided at Mount Vernon. The difference with England soon began, and my father, ready to fly to arms, wished to follow General Washington into battle. But the prayers of his mother and the pleas and caresses of his wife had the power to alter his determination. He sacrificed the wish his heart had burned to gratify and was satisfied to exchange glory for happiness. After eighteen months, my parents' union was blessed with a daughter, who was the first pledge of love such as few can feel—but while her fond parents gazed upon her each day with new delight, she was attacked by a violent illness and died. To relieve my mother's distress, her husband cared for her unremittingly, and he carried her with his mother to visit General Washington, then encamped near Boston. They passed a pleasant time, although they were often alarmed with fears of the British, whose bombs burst frequently over their place of residence. My mother's situation required her return to her father's home, where a year after the birth of their first child I came to assuage her loss. It would have been better had I died as did my sister—but fate decreed otherwise, and my fond parents weaned me with the partiality that parents feel. I had the smallpox, I was attacked by the whooping cough—but I was not destined to die till sufferings more terrible should make my very existence a burden.

Sixteen months after my birth, my sister Patty, now Mrs. Peter, came along, and another sixteen months later, my sister Nelly, now Mrs. Lewis, came to gladden the hearts of her friends, of which she has always had many more than myself. Soon after my brother was born, my father purchased the house in Arlington; he established his home in a handsome style, and it became the seat of hospitality. He loved his family more with each succeeding year, and he was

[148]

adored by his servants and admired by all who saw him; those that knew him considered themselves honored by the acquaintance. My noble father, you were the embodiment of all that was good in man, and the honest pride spent in recounting your merits makes me exult in the reflection that I am worthy to be your daughter.

All genteel strangers found themselves made welcome in my father's house. Among the number was an English physician named Rumney, who played well on the flute and took delight in making me sing. I soon attained a great deal of excellence in singing, and I was always hoisted onto the dinner table to sing for my father's guests. I had a good memory and learned many songs. My father and Dr. Rumney taught me many improper ones, and I can now remember standing on the table, when not more than three or four, singing songs which I did not understand while my father and other gentlemen rolled in their chairs with laughter. I wanted so badly to give him delight. The servants in the passage would join in the fun, and I, holding my head erect, would strut about the table to receive the praises of the guests. My mother remonstrated me in vain—and her husband always said his little daughter could not be punished for what she did not understand. He had no boy of age yet, and I was to make fun for him until my brother grew older. My father would kiss my mother to make peace and, when he would give me a nod, my voice (which was uncommonly powerful even then) resounded throughout the house; my mother, who could not help laughing, had to leave me to the gentlemen, where my father's caresses made me think well of myself. Think me not vain—all who saw me then know I had an uncommonly fine voice for so young a girl.

I was the darling of my Grandmother Washington. She had all the tenderness of manner that my father possessed, and when with her, I was always in her arms. My heart almost broke when she was obliged to go to the general—I was always talking of her and wishing of her return.

Many things occurred at that early period of my life which made an indelible impression. One event that I have never forgotten was the time I was going with the other children into a house where the Negroes picked cotton. I took a cottonseed and put it up my nose. That night I suffered great pain, but my father reproached me for complaining. I stifled my groans and lay in bed with much misery until morning, when he called me to him and, after many efforts, got out the seed. Then he said with sternness, "You have kept me awake and distressed both your parents by doing this; now I will punish you to prevent your acting thus again." He laid me across his knee and whipped me severely. When he put me down, my proud heart swelled with anger—I did not mind the pain he inflicted, but he had disgraced me in front of the other children for a circumstance which had injured me. Had he spoken but one kind word, I should have been subdued—but I thought it was unjust. I felt he had degraded me, and I resolved never to incur humiliation again. I do not recall his punishing me after this time.

Another event marked the color of my future life. A Doctor William Reid of South Carolina spent some time at my Grandfather Calvert's, where a relation of his lived. My sister Patty was the pet of the Calverts, and Dr. Reid was fond of her. But on my own arrival he became much more partial to me. I was but four years old, and he said I was the most interesting child it had ever been his pleasure to encounter. I took an equal fancy to him immediately. We took walks together, he read me books, I would sit on his knee and sing for him. Often when my nurse came to take me to bed, she would find me asleep with my little arms entwined around his neck—the man could not leave me for a moment.

When he was obliged to return to Carolina, he delayed

his departure as long as possible, for, fearing he would go, I would not leave his side at all. Clinging round his neck, I would beg earnestly that he did not take his leave. He was much affected by my distress—he said he wished I were sixteen, as he feared some cold-hearted wretch would one day make his darling miserable. But finally Dr. Reid went away, avoiding saying farewell to me, and I was frantic as I ran around the house in a frenzy, trying to follow him on his journey. I was so much afflicted with longing for him that I became quite sick. The family tried to console me, but in vain, and they could only restrain my tears by telling me that my friend would soon return. My little sisters stood round and offered to comfort me: "Don't cry—he will come back again." It was repeated by all—but it was a long time before I regained tranquility.

My father contemplated this affair with much concern. "God grant, my child, that I may live to protect you," he said. "With feelings as ardent and uncontrollable as mine, I foresee plainly that you, too, will suffer greatly. The proud spirit which breaks forth tells me that my daughter will never do a mean or dishonorable thing—but I fear she will be miserable." His words were of course prophetic. My father was soon to be snatched from his wife and children. Had he lived, I perhaps might have been happy.

My father was ardently devoted to the cause of his oppressed country and, except for the reason assigned, would have been foremost among her defenders. He sang all the revolutionary songs and used to talk of tar and feathers for the Tories, and I imitated him in these pursuits. Whenever my father could, he went to the army, and when the siege of York was nearly concluded, he hurried to see the surrender of Cornwallis. I recollect well how averse he seemed to set off, returning several times to bid his family farewell. I was sick in bed, for he came to the side of it, kissed and blessed me a number of times, and tore himself away. Alas, it was fate's decree that he should never return, and I was the only one of his children who saw him after that day. He arrived at the camp of Washington and saw the British humbled before him, but the camp fever assailed him, and his mother and wife were summoned to attend him.

I was their companion, and I was most grieved to see the late blooming face of my beloved father so changed that I should not have known him. All was done that medical skill and fond affection could perform to save him. Mother never left his side—his eyes were fastened on her. His love for her never changed. It was hard to die so young—he was no more than twenty-seven years old when the end came and tore him from the world which he had adored. When told my father was no more, I insisted upon seeing him, and my nurse went with me into the room, but my mother deterred us at the door. I waxed indignant and said they had no right to prevent my seeing him. I called upon him to return to me and said I supposed my mother would marry someone else but that no other man should be *my father*. I well recollect the grief of my mother and grandmother, and our traveling up the country again, with them all clad in black.

My father's generous soul had made him too little attentive to financial concerns; he had never been brought up with any knowledge of business. He had made bad bargains and had greatly injured his estate—he sold some of the best lands in the state and received little in return. My mother was twenty-five and of a gay turn and high spirits, which had been nurtured by a life of unending prosperity. Before a very long time, she became quite resigned to her loss and began to mingle with a world which always (to her last day) admired her. Still in the full bloom of beauty, with an ample fortune of her own, she was sought by all who wished to secure happiness or fortune. She attracted admiration wherever she appeared—mounted on a fine horse, which she rode skillfully, she was certainly a captivating sight. I mourned for my father and wondered how it was that she could forget him. I am convinced that had I been so well-beloved by such a charming husband, I should have followed him into the grave within a year's time. However, it is most fortunate that my dear mother is so different from me, and I wish no one so ill as to feel so deeply, so durably as I do. . . .

Two years after my father's departure, my mother gave her hand to Dr. Stuart—she chose the man whom she believed would make the best guardian to her children. Dr. Stuart was not then the gloomy gentleman he since became. He had returned from Europe, where he had received every advantage of education, and was the most learned man of his day, a man of respectable family and a character free from reproach. He had studied the profession of medicine, and I believe that he was well qualified to make a conspicuous figure in that art. My mother's friends disapproved of the match, as the man had little fortune, but she was as usual independent of them—finding herself incapable of managing her own property, or that of her children, she was determined to marry Dr. Stuart and make him her husband and the guardian of her children's fortune.

My youngest sister, Nelly, and my brother were sent to reside in Mount Vernon with my grandmother and General Washington—and now my heart sustained yet another pang. The old woman who had nursed my father and all his children was sent to take care of the youngest ones, who needed her. But I was her favorite, and I felt much affection for her. She wept over me in parting, and soon after the wagon which carried her away left, I started out after it, till I had to be brought back by force. Again I was thrown into a fit of melancholy over the loss of someone dear to me.

My mother was pained that I loved her less than my Grandmother Washington. Patty was of a different turn—she was the favorite of my mother's family, of whom I was less fond. An old lady, the aunt of Doctor Reid, idolized me, and when in that house I was generally at her side. Being, like other old maids, very positive, she could not bear it that the others should prefer Patty to myself. She declared to all who would listen that I was worth a dozen Pattys. She would cry when I was sent off—she said she had never seen so charming a child—and when I was with her, every word I uttered was noted as an indication of extraordinary genius. I must admit, however, that the baneful passion of envy was deep in my soul, and while I loved my sister Patty, I always felt that I was of less interest to the Calverts than she was, just as with my grandmother and the general it was Nelly and my brother who were of prime importance. Still, Patty and I were constantly together in those days, as unalike as we were and have continued to be. Patty was, fortunately for herself, created like other people, and she has passed a happy life, while I have been miserable for most of my days.

We were taught our letters to spell and read by my mother and a Miss Allen, a cousin of Dr. Reid, who lived at Mount Airy. I made extraordinarily rapid progress, the family said, and the compliments bestowed upon my capacity led me to learn even more prodigiously than before. When I was eight years old, soon after my mother's second marriage, my half sister, now Mrs. Robinson, joined our family—the first of some twelve children my mother and Dr. Stuart produced. The servants of the house enticed me to feel some jealousy by making me observe my mother's fondness for her new infants. When these unpleasant thoughts would arise, I would think of my Grandmother Washington and Mammy Molly, my old Negro nurse, who always overwhelmed me with caresses when I visited Mount Vernon, although these visits were not as frequent as I should have desired them to be.

My stepfather tried to give us every advantage, and he had a music teacher brought in for us. At a precocious age, I was given *The Spectator* to read, and Dr. Stuart remarked that I was an extraordinary child and would, if a boy, have cut a brilliant figure. I told the tutors to teach me every subject they had knowledge of, and I protested because I thought it unjust that they would not teach me Greek and Latin because I was a girl. They laughed and said that women ought not to know such things, that mending and writing and arithmetic and music was all that I could be permitted to learn.

I have thought of this often with deep regret, and even then I commenced to despise those acquirements which were considered inferior to the masculine ones. My tutor, Old Tracy, held singing in contempt, and the talent which had afforded so much pleasure to my father was laid aside. I never sang again except for myself. I had not one whit of respect for that unpleasant old tutor, who told me viciously conceived lies about my lamented father, and I treated the man with contempt, and even Patty joined me in tormenting him. I acquired great skill in arithmetic and a proficient handwriting, and as Old Tracy excelled in both of these areas, I resolved to surpass him in both. Without any assistance I did the most difficult sums and resolved questions that he tried to vex me with, and I wrote what he had to acknowledge was better than his own. Then I asked him with all the dignity I could assume what right he had to command me who could learn all in half the time and play in the rest. I used to run to another room, and I would lean out the window upon the seat and look back to the time when my father was living and I used to play on the grass in front of him. I was not happy—my mother had an ever-increasing set of Stuart children, and Patty and I were kept very strictly, although she could escape to our Grandfather Calvert's house, where, as I have said, she could do no wrong.

Dr. Stuart was kind to us, but he was not our father. Our one pleasure was going two days every week to dancing school. I was sick when the master first came to instruct us— my sister made some progress, and I heard everyone praise her and became impatient to be well so that I might dance too. I recovered, and after a few lessons, it was easy to dance well. I became the best dancer in the school and was always pleased to be at the head of the class. I not only danced well but conducted myself properly, never interfered with others, and treated the master with respect. It was at the dancing school that I formed an acquaintance with Maria Moxer—we were the same age—and was placed next to her in the dance. She yielded the post of honor without contention or regret, and the affection I felt for her rewarded me with hers. My sister Nelly, too, went to the same school, and she liked many girls, while my attachment was confined solely to Maria. On entering the room we met with joy, and taking hands and embracing each other, we seated ourselves and I took no notice of anyone else till we were called to dance. Afterwards, we resumed our seats; as we always sat together, when then roll was called, our conversation was not interrupted. The other girls called me proud, but they said nothing else about me, for I never did them any injury or said a single word to wound their feelings. I began to despise the days away from the dancing school, the days spent with the irksome Tracy. Though I learned with ease, I despised my tutor.

The election of General Washington to the presidency was a cause of regret to himself and of much pain to the family. It would take from us our grandmother, sister, and brother, and our old nurse, too—my heart was filled with sorrow. We had visited Mount Vernon, where I was always most happy to be in the arms of my grandmother. In those last days I never left my grandmother's side except to roam around with my beloved old nurse. I remember clearly what it was that I felt when the Negroes came to take leave of their mistress, my grandmother—they bid her farewell and blessed her for all her goodness toward them. I can see them even now—many bent down with various infirmities, their heads, grayed by time, uncovered as they bowed down and said, "God bless you all," as the carriage drove off. How pleasant the ride had been, but it was to carry me home and the next day my grandmother was to leave me. I did not sleep that entire night, and the next morning I saw them depart with agonies which to recount at this distance still make my heart ache.

The event was of serious injury to my health, and, to, speak the truth, I have not been of sturdy constitution since. When my grandmother and General Washington departed, I fell ill with a nervous fever. Mammy Molly had to be summoned to nurse me, and I suffered with much distress. I was melancholy, lamenting the loss of my friends. The greatest pleasure I enjoyed was to receive their letters and answer them. One of the few jests ever perpetrated by the general was at my expense. With my characteristic impulsiveness I wrote the president that the dearest wish of my heart was to have his portrait, to which he rejoined that my request should be gratified, although he could not think that the fondest desire of a young girl's heart was to possess the portrait of an old man. However, the miniature was painted; the back of the case was pure enamel, and in an opening bordered with pearls is a lock of General Washington's hair. To this day, it is my most prized possession—of course, I am a woman of very little means.

The general became so ill that his life was despaired of,

and we all felt much distress till assured of his survival. The
Guardian Angel of America preserved her godlike hero, and
the time approached when we were again to see those most
dear to us. My grandmother's footman came on the day
before they arrived to say they were near. My mother was
then confined with one of her later children, and Patty and I
were half crazy for joy—when the carriage stopped, I could
scarcely stand. I wept for joy. My grandmother and the
children came out first, and then my dear old nurse; all
wondered at my growth. Then came the president, and I was
proud to be admired by him. My heart bid me to fly to meet
him, but how could I walk across—I hesitated and blushed,
but my grandmother said, "Go, my darling, or the general
will think you do not love him." That remark gave me
strength to reach his chair, and his arms supported me, timid
as I was. That night I was in great trouble at being obliged to
sit at the head of the table in my mother's absence—extreme
sensibility and a retired life had given me the diffidence
which was remarked on by all who saw me. It was painful to
me when strangers gazed at me, and I could not eat at dinner.
The general said that although he thought a young girl
looked best when blushing, he was still concerned to see me
suffer so much.

My grandmother asked my mother to let her carry me
home with her, and I went with pleasure, yet the tear be-
dewed my cheek when I went to bid my mother farewell.
We were to meet again in a few weeks, yet when I saw her
pale and feeble, my heart was filled with sorrow. She urged
me to go, but the pleasure I felt in being with my grandmother was dampened by the thought that my mother was
absent and not well, and I did not feel happy till she joined
us at Mount Vernon with the babies. We were all happy
together for several months—it was the happiest period of
my life since my beloved father's passing. But soon another

circumstance occurred to give pain.

I have remarked that my father's generous soul had made him regardless of money, while his ignorance of business exposed him to injury from bad men—it was found that the bargain he had made for Abingdon would be ruinous to his children. He had sold valuable estates for paper money, and the sort he was paid in was of no value. Dr. Stuart had been zealously engaged in extricating the estates from embarrassment, and he was advised to give up that place rather than hold it and be subject to a suit which might take all the personal property—my father died without a will, and the laws of that time gave all lands to the male heir when no will existed, so the girls could have only a portion of the personal estate. My mother wished to save a fortune for her daughters and resolved to relinquish a residence to which she was much attracted and bury herself in solitude. She made a great sacrifice for us. The place to which she was to go was one Dr. Stuart had purchased with the wish which all people have when they acquire property, but Dr. Stuart was unqualified to deal with one of the most deceitful men I ever heard of. The place had nothing to recommend it and was twenty miles from Alexandria.

It was during the next years that I feel I truly blossomed—John Adams told the general that I was a fine, blooming, rosy girl and that I had more to recommend me than my sister Nelly. Nelly, of course, was always central to the lives of the general and my grandmother, but I have never begrudged her this—I had more time with our father than she did, owing to my age, and the general looked upon her as a daughter which he was not privileged to have himself.

At seventeen my sister Patty became engaged to Thomas Peter—everyone believed it to be a sober and suitable match. The elders approved, and Mrs. Peter's happy marriage has

borne out the rightfulness of their approval. I became
envious, being Patty's senior, and I sighed over my own state
of spinsterhood. I was advised to not look for perfect
felicity before I consented to wed. But I conceived from
the tales of the poets that the married state was heaven taking its abode on earth. Since then I have learned that, while
love is a mighty pretty thing, like all other delicious things
it is cloying, and when the first transports of passion subside,
which they assuredly always do, it serves to evince that love
is too dainty a food to live upon alone. But these sober
reflections yielded themselves too late to do me any service.

At one time my sisters feared that an attachment would
be formed between myself and Joseph Alston, who made
such a dashing figure in his uniform. They believed he was a
rascal who would cause me only woe, and I acquiesced to
the judgments of others—but Mr. Alston has made a loving
and faithful husband to Aaron Burr's daughter Theodosia,
and again fate had quite other designs upon me.

It was at my grandmother's house at Mount Vernon that
I first laid eyes upon Thomas Law—he had just emigrated
from India, where he had made his fortune, and he brought
to America with him the three half-Asiatic sons of his first
marriage, which ended with the sudden and mournful passing of his wife. He was nearly twenty years older than I, and
he impressed me as a man of great character. I probably
should have realized that he was even then one of the strang-
est men I have ever met. With all good nature and benevo-
lence, his ruling passion was to serve everyone—this kept him
perpetually busy about others. But he paid me much attention, and I was greatly flattered.

We had pleasant walks in the garden, and he talked to
me of his life in India and of England before that. His grandfather and father were both clergymen, and when he was
twelve his father was named Lord Bishop of Carlisle. Being

the fifth of nine children, he was of a restless nature, and at the age of seventeen he entered the service of the East India Company as a writer—the lowest rung of the ladder. In ten years he was Collector of Bahar, where he garnered a fortune of fifty thousand pounds. Such a sum seemed limitless to me. His health, like my own, had been impaired—his from the unwholesome climate of India—and he decided to return to England. His family fortunes did not suffer while he was in the East—his father had died after a much-honored life, one brother was a bishop, another was in parliament, and yet another had become successively the attorney-general, the Lord Chief Justice, and Baron Ellenborough.

Restlessness such as I have often experienced plagued him in England and Mr. Law emigrated to New York, making a home in that city. He had such splendid ideas—his most avowed purpose was to have a part in the upbuilding of the new Federal City. He was not a handsome person, but he was intense, and the equal intensity in myself which I have always cherished made me decide to accept his proposal of marriage. We announced our engagement in February of 1796, when I was but nineteen and Mr. Law nearing forty.

I do not remember too brilliantly the year of my marriage—it is most odd that scenes from my childhood stand out with far more color and intensity than those of my adult life. I am told I made a handsome bride, and the wedding was filled with the most noble guests—General Washington and Dr. Stuart kissed me, and I thought chiefly of my father being unable to see my happiness. My mother and grand-mother cried, and I danced with my newly acquired Asiatic sons, all striking, accomplished boys nearly as old as myself.

Mr. Law and I settled into a home of great style and luxury on New Jersey Avenue in the new Federal City. We drove the handsomest chariot in town—although I have to admit that there was not very much of a town to set the style in those days.

One reading this might ask why it is that I made so much of the years of my childhood and I gloss so quickly and carelessly over those years which rightfully should be most important in a woman's life, those of marriage and child and home. It is curious that I feel so much closer to the Eliza who dandled on her beloved father's knee than to the Mrs. Law that I once was. I am tired now, and the pain of my adulthood is too onerous to bear even in writing. However, there was one joy which would have overshadowed everything—the birth of my little Eliza during the first year of my marriage. It was a difficult birth and I was much afflicted by pain and hysteria, but when I saw the result of my labor, my heart leaped to the heavens to look upon a child, so like me, created for me to love.

Yet there were many deaths in those early years of my marriage which blighted my happiness. When General Washington died, I thought my heart would break with sorrow, and for five years I was able to be with my dear grandmother in her bereavement until fate took her away from my loving arms as well. It does give me pleasure to think, though, that of all her great-grandchildren it was my Eliza who gave to her the most extreme pleasure.

My husband was a stately yet eccentric man with a penchant for penning *vers de societe*. Our house in the city named after our beloved General Washington was a center of hospitality—I made a properly concerned hostess. Distinguished strangers from all lands, interested in our noble experiment of creating a capital on farm lands, came in great numbers and invariably found their way to our house to be entertained. There were Louis Philippe and Twining and Volney, and so many others my mind reels. I enjoyed the commotion and talked for hours endlessly about subjects which now seem so far removed. These visitors were nothing to me, really—I would have given them all up for some peace with my daughter, but my husband liked his company greatly.

There comes a time in the life of a busy man, it seems to me, when he should stop writing what seems to him and some indulgent friends "poetry." That Thomas Law to this day has not desisted in rhyming is an index to the character of the man. I can see him now, sipping madeira by candle-light, penning some more lines, smirking over his own moldy jests. It pained me that he continued in this even after his own sons had been married and formed their own households, but I could have tolerated this had it not been for the more disgusting and unmentionable vices which my former husband practiced. I have never spoken of these and I never shall, but our marriage was over in a figurative sense after not five years of what should have been connubial bliss.

It was nearly a relief to me, then, when he decided to go to England to raise the funds necessary to build the canal that was to make Georgetown and Alexandria commercial centers. Yet I was of mixed feelings on the matter, and a part of me detested his inconsideration at never having asked me to accompany him. I thought of the good times I might have had among my husband's relatives—the Speaker of the House of Lords, the Bishop of Elphin, Lady Rumboid would have doubtless taken to me once the barriers between our-selves were overcome. But Mr. Law denied me the oppor-tunity to make firm friends in England. Being a self-centered individual, he left me in America, and, as I stated, a part of my nature was glad to be free from him. His business for-tunes had been declining, and he lost amounts of money many would be pleased to acquire. Even then there were sharp tongues wagging, wondering how he who had had the splendor and consequences of an Indian prince could be satisfied with his situation in America—but everyone had to admit that he had a companion with whom a normal man might be happy anywhere.

Having for so long sacrificed my own happiness and satisfaction to wifely duties, I found myself enjoying the liberties which my husband's absence procured for me. I make no excuses now for my conduct—let me say that my father was entirely correct when he prophesized about my strange, tortured, passionate nature. I do not regret what I did; no, not for an instant. For the first time in my life, I was in love—and it seemed to be natural to a woman of my nature to offer proofs of regard which no other in my situation would have dared to give. Yet the gentleman in question removed himself from my life and from this country, and to this day he shrouds in mysterious silence all which concerns himself. Of all the joys I have celebrated, this was nearly the greatest—but of all the sorrows suffered by me, the painful conviction that my lover found me unworthy wounded me more sharply than all the rest. It seems shameful to make such a statement, considering the losses I have grievously suffered, and I should be much ashamed, and yet I am not. . . .

After a year's absence, Mr. Law returned to America to find me in great despair. I told him I no longer wished to play out an untruth on the stage of life for all of our friends to see and informed him that it would be all to the good if we separated. I was not surprised to find him most agreeable. There were rumors about me, and this turned my husband against me. To this day I revile those who have spoken so slanderously about me, although, no doubt ignorant, I continue on good terms with a few of these vicious gossips. They even took my daughter away from me and into the custody of her father.

The settlement concluded between us was such that I

was to receive an annuity of fifteen hundred dollars, and it was with characteristic unpunctuality that I received the first of these payments from Mr. Law—the laxity and slowness has continued, of course, throughout my lifetime and has in large measure contributed to the further impairment of my health.

There was one pleasure to be gained in separation—I elected to call myself Mrs. Custis, retrieving for myself the much-honored name of my father and his father. I was always accepted after my divorce, although in an age of scandal the breath of suspicion could not be expected to spare myself alone. My beloved mother and Dr. Stuart were most distressed by the estrangement between my husband and myself, but they had their own family and their own bonds to share. My mother left the world a less joyous place when she departed to join my father, her first and abiding love, in 1811; Dr. Stuart followed her into the grave not three years after. At least my grandmother and General Washington were spared the knowledge of my marital unhappiness. The general had come to entrust Mr. Law in matters of business, and without doubt my husband's wealth, experience, and family contributed to make even the godlike savior of our nation blind to Mr. Law's faults of vanity, egoism, and bad judgment. In truth, I must state that it was not until my marriage that these (and oh, far worse!) faults came to light as besetting sins.

After we had endured a separation for six years, my husband established residence in Vermont, that state being one of the few where a divorce could be obtained on grounds of incompatibility. Our marriage was dissolved in 1811. By way of celebrating his freedom, that odious man distributed among his new-made New England neighbors the china he had brought back from England, such china that I was to have received as a token of his love. Let those Vermonters keep Law's china! I have not had to endure marriage, and that is

[165]

gift enough for me.

Looking back on it, it is hard to say that there was ever any real companionship on either side of our marriage. I was such a young and foolish girl, easily won over by mature position, wealth, and the ambitious nature of my suitor. And it was perhaps Mr. Law's worship of General Washington and his ambition that led him to seek an alliance with the president's family. Rage for popularity, pride, and vanity were his chief qualities, and when I became so neglected as to wax indignant he turned on me with a malignancy which increased with years of separation—no doubt it will carry on with him to his grave. To the world he would write that he never did impeach my purity of conduct, but he did not pay much tribute to that in our private moments.

For the remaining years of my life I enjoyed always the friendship and companionship of many men and women of distinction, and I believe I have earned their consideration as well. Several times in the past twenty years have I professed myself violently in love, during which times I made known that I was ready to follow my beloved to France or the Siberian wilds, if need be. Tempered by age, I now am able to see what amusement such devotion must have caused on the part of my friends. Yet even now, having reached such an age, I would once again enter the married state if I could find in this world a being who will love me and who can obtain my affections. Then I would become the best of wives, go with the object of my love to the world's end if he should will it—I would devote my whole life to love. But I fear this is not to be my fate and I shall remain as I am now— not happy, but determined to employ all my power to promote the good of others and deserve the blessings of heaven.

The one great interest in these later years has, alas, been my major suffering. I did not see my daughter for many years. I can recollect one meeting when young Eliza was just eighteen—such a beautiful woman she made! I came from Washington to Philadelphia to see my beloved child; she had finished her school studies and was to live, alternately, with two lady friends of Mr. Law's. I was much amazed to find her as tall as I was and stouter than I thought she would be—how well she had improved. I told her then that my fervent prayer was that she might meet with some good, amiable man worthy of such an angel and find in him a friend and protector for life—as I never did. I endured such misery being separated from my daughter. Mr. Law never intended to let me see her, and in this I suffered the most from his enmity, may God forgive the man.

Separated from my child, with a numerous family of relations, all of whom had families, who were all prosperous, who wanted nothing from me, I stood alone in this world, and I stand alone even more sharply today, for my beloved Eliza was taken from me permanently by a force much more powerful than Mr. Law's. Eliza married at twenty. The gentleman she chose was of fair face and good family, Lloyd Rogers of Baltimore. I was not to attend the wedding, and could not share in her happiness. I did visit her (Oh, I am a constant visitor everywhere these days, having no home of my own to speak of) and was blessed with three grandchildren so beauteous that the world has never seen the like before. The eldest daughter was named Eliza, and this grandmother's heart must in truth say that she is my favorite. But my Eliza, my dear daughter, departed this world after only five years of wedded life—too, too short a time for one so radiant and gentle. Has ever an individual had to endure more mourning than I?

Mr. Law's monetary fortunes continued to decline—or so I was constantly told by his representatives. When my son-in-law reproached Mr. Law for not paying my annuity, the man made plea that whereas he once had an income of thirty thousand dollars he had been reduced to five hundred dollars. This may not have been a deception—had I remained as wife, I should have seen to it that money was better handled and not squandered on things such as "splashes" for Maryland farmers. Mr. Law tried so hard to win affection, poor man, he often paid a pretty price for it.

I have been the last three months at the home of my old and dear friend Mrs. Jones. Lately I have not been quite well—an aching head, poor digestion, and much bodily complaint. I would have liked to have led a life of service to my country, as my forebears did—formerly I knew all the public people. But now most in Congress, or the offices, are strangers to me. I have given up general society. I have no power of serving anyone now.

Since I suffered my last and most grievous loss, that of my child, I have been useless. I wished to devote all my remaining energies to the care of my grandchildren, but they too were removed from me by their savage father, my son-in-law, who has now, too, turned against me and wishes me no intercourse with them. A lifelong accumulation of sorrow has destroyed my health and my spirits. I have been confined to my bed more frequently of late. I see no one but my own relations and most particular friends. I do not wish to enter general society again—I have neither health nor spirits to make it desirable, and though I am told otherwise, I venture that I am now forgotten by most. It has been four years now—how much longer, O God, must your poor servant suffer?

Note: On New Year's Day, 1832, Eliza Parke Custis died while on a visit to Richmond. She is buried at Mount Vernon, Virginia.

THE SMILE IN THE CLOSET

Secretly, you see, he was happy.

He would lie awake nights thinking about the rich texture of his life and end up thanking Someone for it. Naturally
he was an atheist, except when it came to this. Who was
responsible for all the good in his life? He couldn't believe in
an anthropomorphic God, and he felt uncomfortable around
words like Fate. Somehow he could not bring himself to
accept all the credit; it was too egotistical, even to himself.
More and more, he came to view his life as an unyielding ser-
ies of lucky breaks. It was as if there were a conspiracy to
make him happy.

They would be surprised if they knew this about him.
In public, he was a genial cynic; he had once taken great
pride in describing himself as "the Compleat Neurotic." Yet
slowly he found himself turning into an intellectual Pollyana,
and he couldn't understand where this had come from.

There was no demarcation line, no DMZ between optimism and pessimism, no date that he could pinpoint as the
time when he had finally decided that the good in life far out-
weighed the bad. There had been, starting in early adoles-
cence, nearly a decade of psychotherapy; there had been a
nervous breakdown somewhere in the middle of that; there
had been a couple of love affairs, much schooling, and various

[169]

events, both external and internal, in the interim. But there was nothing—not family background, nor intellectual influences, nor any subcutaneous religiosity—that could account for his conversion. There was no conscious attempt at Coue; still, he began to feel, in the words of the Beatles' song, that things were getting better all the time.

It was, after all, a radical doctrine. Not radical in the political or cultural sense—that would have been all right. But his sense of optimism, of life progressing along according to some well-constructed and beneficent pattern, was an almost shameful secret; he was afraid of revealing it to others lest they think him crazy, or worse, believe him and then become jealous. It was a similar fear which led him to play the role of the well-meaning scatterbrain; he had found out early in life that people were, in general, more open and more compassionate with a slightly goofy person than they were with a shrewd, intelligent one. He carried out the charade, that of the male equivalent to the dumb blonde, and some people were taken in. Accordingly, he found that to have a positive attitude toward his own life in the latter half of the twentieth century was to be looked upon, at the very least, as illiberal.

The first full-blown daytime attack of good feeling occurred about a month after he had terminated his therapy. The night before he had gone, with friends, to a party sponsored by Bisexual Liberation. It was a dismal affair, with dismal people who seemed to him very sad in their dogged determination to be 'open' and 'free.' There was a toupeed young business man whose wife was home with their infant son; she knew nothing of his homosexual inclinations. There was an overtly neurotic girl from the suburbs, who had brought her husband along; the husband spoke no English but the wife made up for that. The leader of the organization was a psychologist in a loud body shirt that hung over his belly and exposed too much of his chest; this man seemed

[170]

sadder than all the others, even more so because he had lately become a frequent guest on television talk shows. He and his friends left the party early, stopped off for a drink, and agreed that it would have been better had they not spent their money on the donation fee, but instead paid each other three dollars to discuss bisexuality among themselves. Driving home, he began to have perverse thoughts: he realized how much he had loved his old girlfriends, and how much, in a way, he still loved them. When confronted with reality, all his fantasies, homosexual and heterosexual, faded into nothingness. He was satisfied with his life; more than that, he was thrilled with it. He had had relationships with mutual respect, honesty, and communication. The next afternoon, he drove out to the beach; as he walked toward the board-walk, he felt a heavy November wind blowing against him. It was a fiercer wind than he had ever known, and as he managed to make his way to the ocean, he had a crazy thought: that this was the most complete moment of his life. It felt so wonderful that he couldn't bear to stay on the beach for more than a few minutes.

Yet an hour later, he wrote the following, on a sheet of yellow legal paper: "I guess it's about 3 p.m. This has been one of the most incredibly beautiful days of my life. Right now I'm lying on the grass in a suburban state park, feeling better than I can ever remember feeling. About a year ago, Eleanor and I picnicked here. . . . The grass smells so good. The trees here are mostly bare but it seems beautiful, not in spite of their bareness, but because of it. This good feeling won't last—nothing does. But it doesn't matter, because it's here, it does exist now (this paper is a record of that) and it's as real as anything I've ever experienced. . . . Driving up here, I realized what a marvelous thing life is, and how lucky I am to be alive. I stopped at a roadside phone to call my father at his office; I wanted to tell him that I loved him. Why should we have to wait for funerals to express our love? My parents made terrible mistakes in raising me, but their intentions were good and loving. My father wasn't in, so I called mother at home and told her that I loved her. She said she loved me too and that she'd give my father the message. Maybe I had to learn how much I hated my parents before I could see how much I loved them. . . . A leaf just settled near me. It's ripped and brown, but somehow it seems so noble. I let it go to join the other leaves. . . . At the moment I can only feel good things. I feel integrated, whole, sensitive, unique. Drugs could never do this, nor alcohol, nor sex. It's as if, for only an instant, I've discovered the secret of how to live satisfactorily. It can't last—it might be unbearable if it did; I think, thought, that this feeling may return again. No matter what happens to me, I can remember this moment and let it stand as a testament to whatever is good about the world. . . . I've just been jumping from one wooden picnic table to the other. I stopped at one table, and standing, I threw my arms out exultantly toward the sky. I have never, ever, felt so exhilarated. I've been dancing on tables, laughing, acting silly. There's no one around, but I don't think I'd care if they could see me. I did a somersault (a somersault!) and sang out loud. My shirttail's sticking out and I'm rolling in the grass, and I feel great. Maybe I'm crazy, and this is insanity. If so, I want to go completely insane. Now I know what an epiphany is."

It faded away, of course, and in a day, he was anxious about a dinner party he had been invited to. But the feeling did return, less than a month later, at Christmastime. He had gone out for dinner with his family, and witnessed an anxiety attack on the part of his younger sister, who could not stand to be in the restaurant. He knew she was going through the same sort of unbearable tension that he had once gone through. And incredibly, he helped her, when no one else

[172]

could, and this made him feel very good indeed. It was Christmas Eve, and there was a party at a friend's house, someone he had recently met. He realized that he was sure of his feelings that evening; that is, his feelings were confused, but he knew he could trust in them. And this led almost to mania. The Christmas party was relaxed and low-key; again, most of the people seemed somehow sad. They hardly could bring themselves to play charades. The host of the party was distracted, though; not all of the invited guests had shown up, and moreover, his girlfriend had recently left him and this was to be his first Christmas alone. Knowing how much his host dreaded being alone, he stayed there after everyone had left, and watched one of the film versions of "A Christmas Carol" until very late. He left, and suddenly he was aware that he felt very good again, the way he did back in that park the month before. But it seemed even better; life seemed even more worthwhile than before.

From then on, the feelings struck with regularity. There was no one he knew that felt this way, except perhaps for an elderly black woman who had once taught Sunday school; but she was dead now, and he could not ask her if what he felt was similar to what she had felt. Perhaps everyone was a secret life-lover, he thought, but even so, he kept his good feelings to himself. One could only boast of one's sicknesses, after all; to brag about one's health was very bad form indeed. But every night or so he would lie in bed, stay awake until early morning, and gò over his life: the things he had done, the people that he knew, the books he read, the little routines of his existence that gave him a shockingly inordinate amount of pleasure. Sometimes he would try to masturbate to a shameful fantasy, but this rarely worked. Most times he would smile and hug himself gently and thank the Someone and feel perfectly wonderful. By the morning no one would know, and he could be with people and pretend that his life was like theirs, and get even more satisfaction out of his secret vice.

Perhaps, he kept thinking, one day he would go back to normal. But somehow he never did.

SUMMONING ALICE KEPPEL

In those days Canadians were in danger of deteriorating physically. Influenza was a dreaded disease. People either had butlers and maids, or lived in sub-human conditions. The pope played lawn tennis every Wednesday morning. Bustles were just going out. Bicycles popped up everywhere. It was a different era.

Folks our age are inclined to reminisce, says Dean, who was present at the creation. It cannot be denied that if you get enough of us together for a long enough time—say, three successive evenings of playing Scrabble or listening to jazz or eating pizza pies—the subject is bound to come up. Invariably someone will tell you where they were or what they were doing when the Queen summoned Alice Keppel to the palace.

A faint smile draws across Dean's lips. He was seventeen then, and did not yet shave. He wanted to be strong like the young vicar who could pick up entire pews with his teeth. Dean was exercising with his bar-bells when he heard the news. His sister entered the room without knocking, and at first he was embarrassed because he was stripped to the waist. In those days it was not proper for a girl to see her brother's chest. Still, that was all forgotten in the excitement, all forgotten when Dean's sister told him the news. His

[175]

sister said, "She's been summoned . . . Mrs. Keppel," and they
stood in silence for a moment and then began to waltz around
gaily. It didn't matter that Dean didn't have his shirt on, or
that the girl he was dancing with was his sister. Alice Keppel
had been summoned, and a new age had begun.

In his comprehensive study of that era, *The Proud
Flower* (London: Chatto and Windus, 1944), J.H. Lyman
writes: ". . . The event was for millions, not merely the death
of one era and the birth of another; it was not merely a
dramatic happenstance in the lives of the giants of the time;
it was not even a human tragicomedy. The summoning of
Alice Keppel has become, for a generation of men and
women, the culmination of all recorded history . . . it is *their*
mythology, *their* religion, and they guard it as jealously as
the proverbial silver chalice."

A cult has been created from these events, even now it
exists. Marais is the oldest one still alive. "Yes, I worship
Alice Keppel as my god," Marais will tell you. "She was
everything a person should be: charitable, beautiful, generous, spiteful. She achieved perfection."

Others are not so sure. Marais' own nephew, the social
psychologist Yves Boulle-Delmas states: "Frankly, I find the
cult of Alice Keppel to be no more than the coming to the
surface of latent homoerotic desires, specifically those revolv-
ing around the anus. This was no superwoman here, no blushing saint. After all, when you come down to it, what was
Alice Keppel anyway? A mistress, that's all. A mistress who
happened to be summoned to a place that happened to be
the royal palace to appear at the deathbed of a man who
happened to be very important, relatively speaking. You see,
it is not the events themselves which are momentous and awe-
inspiring, but the way in which these events are perceived. To
a certain mind Mrs. Keppel is a god, just as to a certain mind
Jesus is a god, or Marx or Gautama or Kafka. These mental-

ities will always be with us . . . they are no more representative of the collective psyche than a schizophrenic is."

Other folks feel differently. Otherwise how can one explain the fact that so many people, so many charwomen and M.P.s and housewives and bankers and merchants, all stood vigil at the palace, waiting day and night for Alice Keppel to be summoned to the royal deathbed? And when she did finally appear, how can one explain the spontaneous outburst of enthusiasm that greeted her? Lyman quotes one down-to-earth vigil keeper, the hardy trollop Tess Barchester as saying, "That gal's worthy of any respect I can give her. She's a proper champion, she is."

Kerensky was only seven years old when it happened. He remembered the excitement, even though at the time he did not understand what was going on. Still, they let him out of school early, and he was grateful for that.

"I guess today you'd call it charisma," Madelaine says. "God, did she have charisma. Such sang-froid. I guess most of us girls worshipped her, tried to emulate her style." (At this point Madelaine shakes her head ruefully.) "Not that any of us could achieve it. Of course by then I was a demi-vierge and a bit too old for the whole thing. Or at least I thought I was. But when I heard she was being summoned, I broke down and cried with the rest of the girls."

Lyman notes one of the ironies of history: "At the precise moment of the summons to the deathbed, another man was dying a continent away. That man was Winslow Homer, by that time America's most renowned painter. The doctors said nothing more could be done for him, and so his family stood by the bedroom door around the clock. When the news of Alice Keppel came, an argument ensued between various members of the dying artist's family. Some cautioned that telling him the news would speed his demise, while the others argued that Homer, as an aesthete, would want to be

[177]

told. Before the latter faction could prevail, the great artist died quietly in his sleep, never to know the fate of Alice Keppel and the King."

Francis thought it was a joke at first: "We had just finished morning mass, and up comes the aged cleaning-woman with this incredible story about Alice Keppel. Well! We all burst out laughing, telling her, 'Mollie, have you been at the Monsignor's brandy again?' and 'Mollie, you shouldn't say things like that, not in a house of God!' But an hour later we knew that Mollie had been telling the truth. . . . I still don't know why we didn't take her seriously at first. But then, we were very naive then. The world was a naive place then."

The students at Tuskegee Institute took the news stoically, almost casually. "I have the feeling," one was quoted by Lyman as saying, "that this is only the beginning." Prophetic reactions aside, the students voted not to close down the school, feeling instead that Alice Keppel would have wanted them to continue their education. They wore violet armbands, though, to honor the daughter of their idol.

Leonard's wife went completely mad when she heard the news of the summons. She had a total breakdown and lay in bed for days, listening to the birds singing in Greek and imagining that Alice Keppel and the King were lurking in the azaleas and using the foulest possible language. Years later, Leonard's wife recovered her sanity and wrote a panegyric to her lover, who was also the lover of Alice Keppel's daughter. Unfortunately, the manuscript has since been destroyed.

Of all the film versions of the incident, the public most enjoyed *The Magnificent Mistress*, with Sylvia Sidney. Many film buffs (at least those who subscribe to the auteur theory) prefer Howard Hawks' *A Day In June*, with Jane Wyman. And yet there are those who swear by *The Alice Keppel Story*, with Carole Lombard.

A young Guggenheim was going to meet the Carpathia when she got word of the summons. She was so startled that she did not even notice that it was not her mother, but her father's mistress, who was descending the gangplank with her father. The family talked of nothing else for years.

There are people today, it is said, who have never heard of Alice Keppel or the summons to the palace. This saddens one, but it cannot be helped. Recently a semi-official newspaper in the Middle East had a front page editorial condemning those "who would raise to the level of historical fact blatantly fanciful fairy-stories concerning a certain royal mistress."

Yet hundreds of tourists pass by the Alice Keppel Memorial every week to pay their respects to this gallant woman. And millions more remember the joy she brought to them, albeit for a brief moment in eternity. Granted, there will always be those malcontents and disgruntled and ignorant people to whom the words "Alice Keppel's summons" will mean no more than some woman getting a parking ticket. Of these people, however, it is best to take no notice. There are plenty of better people to talk to.

DIARRHEA OF A WRITER

*A Musing on the Occasion
of the Publication
of My 75th Short Story*

Richard G.   Class 2-1

The Biggest Bear

A boy named Johnny Orchard wanted a bear-skin
for his barn. He didn't get a bear-skin, but he found
a baby bear instead. Johnny fed the bear every day
until he became the biggest bear in the woods. His
father said he should get rid of the bear. When
Johnny would let the bear in the woods, he would
always come back.

One day, Johnny tied the bear to himself and
took him into the woods to be shot. As he was about
to load the gun, the bear ran off with Johnny. There
was a bear trap nearby and they both fell in. The
bear was taken to the New York Zoo. Now Johnny
goes to visit him often.

A- writing is too sloppy

I have wanted to be a writer for a long time.

Miss Gura, my second-grade teacher, wasn't too good at
spotting misplaced modifiers or missing antecedents, but she
had a sharp eye for what was neat and what was not—at least
in terms of penmanship.

[180]

Today *I* am a teacher of bright-eyed pharmacy students. I am supposed to be teaching these future druggists to write effective sentences and coherent paragarphs. We do not worry about penmanship at all.

Mostly they are dismal writers. But occasionally I get one or two in a class who are born writers. Now that I have used the phrase *born writers*, I have to admit that I don't know what it means. When I ask myself if I was/am a "born writer," I can't answer that. The urge has always been strong, often the words have been weak and unwilling.

This morning, one of my born writers came to see me after class. A charming kid, well-liked, nice-looking: he's a prefectionist and wanted to check with me on some very obscure points of footnoting and bibliography. John is writing a term paper on escapology; he is a magician himself, and modestly tells me that he made over $2500 from performing his magic last year. I do not tell him that I do not make much more than that for teaching four sections of freshman composition a year in the pharmacy school. There is no need.

After I have consulted with Dean Spector about whether the proper bibliographic form requires the writing out or the abbreviation of a month in a periodical's date (an issue I couldn't care less about), John and I begin talking about writing and *his* writing in particular.

"How would you say I am as a writer?" John asks me.

I think. "You're probably the best in the class."

John looks at me for a minute and tells me that his teacher from last term suggested he think about going into writing as a career. Professor Malley thought John's journal entries were funnier than anything in *The National Lampoon*. Instinctively, I know Professor Malley was right. John *is* good. But what he wanted to know was whether I thought he could make it as a writer.

"Yeah," I hear myself saying to John, "I think you could make it. But stick with it here and get your pharmacy degree so—"

"—I'll have something to fall back on." Of course he knows the words. We both smile.

After a second I say, "I wish *I* had something to fall back on."

"You're a teacher," John tells me.

I don't say anything.

In the afternoon I come home to find in the mail a new little magazine with a story of mine contained therein. It is always sweet to savor my own words in typeface, even in a mimeo mag. As usual, I have to fight my embarrassment to read my own words, but I find the story—for I call my things "stories"—is better that I remember it. Of course it is still second-rate, even though it gets me to laugh out loud once. But that is all right, I think. It's there in print.

No rejections today. One acceptance. The editor is a sort-of-friend, but his letter is matter-of-fact. I wonder: is he taking the story because of friendship, or because he doesn't want to hurt my feelings, or because he thinks I have a "name." But that is all right, too. It will be there in print in a few months and I can get that same sweet feeling once more.

A letter from Otterbein College, a school to which I have applied. I belong to the Associated Writing Programs, receive their job placement newsletter, respond to all openings for which I am even remotely qualified. I open the envelope: good rag paper inside. The letter: "It has not been an easy job trying to select ten candidates out of a pool of well over 200!" Dear Dr. Bulthaup, Vice President for Academic Affairs—the exclamation point was a clever touch, endearing. "Fortunately, we have been able to accomplish this task and regret to inform you. . . . "

Regret is all you really need to read in some letters. Often I think it is one of the most useful words in modern English. But this is really all right, too. It's not Dr. Bulthaup's fault. And who really wanted to leave New York City for Westerville, Ohio? Besides, I never expect to get any of the jobs I apply for. Only four days ago I had gotten regrets from the Chairman of the English Department at the University of Maryland-Baltimore County, the Dean of Communications Arts at Pepperdine University, and the Head of the Writing Program at MIT. I don't even give myself the satisfaction of keeping these letters. Into the garbage pail they go.

After watching "my" soap opera, I go over to the copy center downtown and have my latest story and my latest acceptance notice xeroxed. I keep a record of my acceptances in a loose-leaf binder. I keep xeroxed copies of my published stories in a file cabinet; some of them I send out to friends who would not otherwise see the magazines I appear in. It's an expense, but at least it gives me the feeling that I'm communicating with someone.

Very rarely a stranger will write me, someone who has read one of my stories in some little mag. Two weeks ago I received a wonderful letter from a man in Texas. "Fame and fortune are coming your way," he wrote me. "This is my first fan letter so please excuse my awkwardness." I excused him a thousand times and sent him a letter saying there were better people he could be writing to. I also sent him xeroxed copies of several other of my stories. He hasn't written back so I assume he took my advice.

Joey, the muscular kid who works part-time at the copy center, hands me back my collated copies. Lately Joey has taken to xeroxing an extra copy of my stories for himself.

[183]

This embarrasses me, and Joey knows it, so this is something that we never discuss. "Have a good day, Richie," he tells me as I hand him what I owe.

On the way downstairs I meet someone I sort of know, another guy caught in the English Ph.D. glut. He mentions seeing a story of mine in proofs—it is a story in the college magazine where he teaches; one of his students is the fiction editor. "It was good," he says. I change the subject because I remember that piece and how personal it was and how to make it sound real I used my real name and revealed things which now embarrass me. I wrote that I was having a homosexual affair with a student. *Why do I write things like that?*

I hurry away as quickly as is politely possible.

At home, I think about writing for little magazines. I get out my list of stories and discover that today's is my 75th. Wow. Even my girlfriend, I think, must be secretly impressed. I must be hot shit, right?

Wrong.

Most of the time I doubt that I have any talent whatsoever. I tell myself that talent isn't important, but then what's left? Perseverance? Persistance? Old-fashioned stubbornness? Just yesterday I was in one of my thrice-weekly Great Depressions, brought on, as usual, by the ever-more-clear conviction that I Cannot Write. To further flagellate myself, I went to Brentano's and spent an hour going through the latest *O. Henry Prize Stories*, calculating how many of my pieces the editors must have read and—justifiably—overlooked. I glance at the winning stories and assure myself these people have something I do not. And then I wander over to my neighborhood branch library to continue to assure myself of my worthlessness. Philip Roth had a story in *Epoch* when he was 23 that got into the Martha Foley *Best American Short Stories* anthology? Maria Katzenbach, class of '77, mind you, has a novel out on the shelves?—and she was on *Today* too, holding her own with Tom Brokaw and Gene Shalit. Don't even *mention* Rafael Yglesias—does the dust jacket say he wrote the book when he was *fifteen*?

And the editor of *The Literary Review* twists the knife in nicely with a pointed rejection of two of my stories. "You are a prolific lightweight," he writes. "Most of this is written diarrhea."

Diarrhea. I sort of know what he's getting at: my stories are not so much solid things as dribs and drabs and noise, brief explosions. I have no sense of plot. I use the first-person subject pronoun way too much. Sometimes I wince at my own dialogue. Nothing ever seems to come out the way I had intended it to, there in my imagination, before I ever hit the first key of my Smith-Corona.

I make resolutions. *I will try to write a well-constructed Jean Stafford story. I will write less, not force myself to. I will write nothing but third-person prose about characters who do not resemble me at all.* And like an ornery dieter, my resolutions make me unhappy; so I break all of them.

My friend George, who is a fiction writer and a poet, always seems so self-confident in his letters. He is younger and less-published than I, yet still he can refer to his "work" without sounding the least sheepish or apologetic. When George wrote me that I was his "favorite fiction writer," I was horrified. *I'm not even a writer*, I wanted to scream. Seventy-five short stories in little magazines, an M.F.A., the seal of approval from Poets & Writers—that doesn't mean anything. Saul Bellow is a writer. Norman Mailer is a writer. Jorge Luis Borges, for God's sakes, is a writer. I can't call myself that—not yet.

So I have a curious ambivalence about the stories I've had published in little magazines and small presses. On the one hand, I'm proud of my accomplishments, proud of being tough enough to stand Himalayas of rejections, proud of being able to stick it out in college teaching for nearly no money, proud of the words I have written. Yet I live in New York and read the *New York Times Book Review* every Sunday morning, and I have friends who get paid more than I earn in a year for a single piece in *The New Yorker*. I yearn to be part of that world and am just as sure I never can be. But it's all right, as I said.

Last February the National Arts Club held a dinner honoring Saul Bellow at which he was presented with their annual Literary Medal. I scraped together $45 for two tickets for me and my best friend Linda, an editor at *Seventeen*. It was a black-tie affair, very stodgy yet very glamorous. Malamud and Cheever were there. Dick Cavett. Tom Guinzberg of Viking Books. Real literary people. Linda and I made our way to the couch where Bellow was being sought out. She got his autograph. I opened with a halfway-clever remark I had memorized for a week, a line based on one of his more obscure writings, to show him that I wasn't just another culture vulture. Then I stammered: "I know this sounds silly . . . but your books mean a lot to me." I could have died, I was being so banal. And he was uncomfortable, too. We chatted for another minute about the rain and Jerusalem and Chicago, and finally I managed to get out: "I'm trying to be a fiction writer, too." He nodded, and I practically ran away. There were plenty of other people crowding him to take my place.

Standing by Linda in the corner of what was once Governor Tilden's palatial home, I felt completely humiliated. And yet I thought about all the questions I really wanted to ask him. *Did you ever doubt yourself? How do you know when you've written something important? Did you ever want to give up?*

Suddenly I noticed Saul Bellow coming my way. He was going past me, to talk to Dick Cavett, but there was a moment when he was about to get real close. And he asked me: "What did you say your name was again?"

I was in heaven. I babbled out four syllables, managing not to make a mistake.

"I'll look for you," said the winner of the 1976 Nobel Prize for literature. He then passed me by.

Here I am, Mr. Bellow. *Where* I don't know. My writing is too sloppy. This may be diarrhea. But I'm in print, and that's almost enough for now.

Richard Grayson, 1981.